THE TEMPLAR DETECTIVE

AND THE PARISIAN ADULTERESS

A TEMPLAR DETECTIVE THRILLER

Also by J. Robert Kennedy

James Acton Thrillers

The Protocol
Brass Monkey
Broken Dove
The Templar's Relic
Flags of Sin
The Arab Fall
The Circle of Eight
The Venice Code
Pompeii's Ghosts
Amazon Burning
The Riddle
Blood Relics
Sins of the Titanic
Saint Peter's Soldiers
The Thirteenth Legion

Raging Sun
Wages of Sin
Wrath of the Gods
The Templar's Revenge
The Nazi's Engineer
Atlantis Lost
The Cylon Curse
The Viking Deception
Keepers of the Lost Ark
The Tomb of Genghis Khan
The Manila Deception
The Fourth Bible
Embassy of the Empire
Armageddon
No Good Deed

Special Agent Dylan Kane Thrillers

Rogue Operator
Containment Failure
Cold Warriors
Death to America
Black Widow

The Agenda
Retribution
State Sanctioned
Extraordinary Rendition
Red Eagle

The Messenger

Templar Detective Thrillers

The Templar Detective
The Parisian Adulteress
The Sergeant's Secret

The Code Breaker
The Black Scourge
The Unholy Exorcist

The Lost Children

Kriminalinspektor Wolfgang Vogel Mysteries

The Colonel's Wife   *Sins of the Child*

Delta Force Unleashed Thrillers

Payback   *Kill Chain*
Infidels   *Forgotten*
The Lazarus Moment   *The Cuban Incident*

Detective Shakespeare Mysteries

Depraved Difference   *Tick Tock*   *The Redeemer*

Zander Varga, Vampire Detective

The Turned

THE TEMPLAR DETECTIVE

AND THE PARISIAN ADULTERESS

J. ROBERT KENNEDY

UnderMill PRESS

Copyright ©2018 J. Robert Kennedy

ISBN: 9780991814282

First Edition

For Ian Kennedy.
Not only family, but one of my biggest supporters.

THE TEMPLAR DETECTIVE AND THE PARISIAN ADULTERESS

A TEMPLAR DETECTIVE THRILLER

THE
TEMPLAR
DETECTIVE

AND THE

PARISIAN
ADULTRESS

A TEMPLAR DETECTIVE

THRILLER

"A Templar Knight is truly a fearless knight, and secure on every side, for his soul is protected by the armor of faith, just as his body is protected by the armor of steel. He is thus doubly armed, and need fear neither demons nor men."

Bernard de Clairvaux, c. 1135
De Laude Novae Militae—In Praise of the New Knighthood

"If a man is found lying with the wife of another man, both of them shall die, the man who lay with the woman, and the woman."

Deuteronomy 22:22

AUTHOR'S NOTE

This is the second novel in this series, and for those who have read the first and embraced these characters as so many of you have, please feel free to skip this note, as you will have already read it in the first novel.

The word "detective" is believed to have originated in the mid-nineteenth century, however, that doesn't mean the concept of someone who investigated crime originated less than two hundred years ago. Crime long pre-dated this era, and those who investigated it as well.

The following historical thriller is intended to be an entertaining read for all, with the concept of a "Templar Detective" a fun play on a modern term. The dialog is intentionally written in such a way that today's audiences can relate, as opposed to how people might have spoken in Medieval France, where, of course, they would have conversed in French and not English, with therefore completely different manners of speaking, and of addressing one another. For consistency, English phrasing is always used, such as Mister instead of Monsieur, for example. This does not mean they will be speaking to each other as rappers and gangsters, but will instead communicate in ways that imply comfort and familiarity, as we would today. If you are expecting, "Thou dost hath offended me, my good sir," then prepareth thyself for disappointment. If, however, you are looking for a fast-paced adventure, with plenty of action, mystery, and humor, then you've come to the right place.

Enjoy.

PREFACE

In 1314, the Kingdom of France was rocked with what became known as the Tour de Nesle Affair. King Philip IV's three daughters-in-law stood accused of adultery by his own daughter, two caught having affairs with Norman knights in the tower known as the Tour de Nesle.

Punishment was swift and brutal.

The men involved were castrated, then drawn and quartered—an excruciating death. The women didn't fare much better. Both had their heads shaved and were sentenced to life in prison. One died under suspicious circumstances shortly after imprisonment, and the other, after eight years, was allowed to serve out the remainder of her sentence in a nunnery, though died within a year from illnesses acquired in prison. The third was placed under house arrest for a year, due to her admission that she had known of the affairs and hadn't reported them.

This left two of the King's three sons without wives, and none with male heirs. After King Philip's death later that year—some say due to the strain of the scandal—each of these sons eventually held power, the next oldest replacing the previous upon death, but ultimately, the last died, and thanks to the affair, the hereditary line was broken, ending over 340 years of Capetian rule.

Though this wasn't the first time scandal had rocked the King's Court…

Paris, Kingdom of France
AD 1297

"Milady, you must leave now!"

Lady Joanne de Rohan stared at her chambermaid, her heart pounding with panic. "But how can I? If I do, he'll take it as proof of my guilt!"

Beatrice urged her to hurry, her discovery of only a short while ago leaving her in a state Joanne had never seen her in, and it was worsening her own. "I heard him, Milady. He's mad with rage! He's calling for your head for the betrayal." She stopped, uncharacteristically grabbing her mistress by both arms. "If he lays hands on you, I fear even the good Lord will be unable to protect you from the evil in the master's heart."

Joanne dropped on the edge of her bed, pulling at her hair. "This entire thing, it makes no sense! I've done nothing wrong!"

Beatrice hauled her to her feet then continued putting together a bundle of essentials. "He cares not of the truth, Milady, only of what he has been told in the message." She shoved the bundle into Joanne's hands. "Milady, you must go, now! I have a horse prepared for you with two days provisions, just in case."

Joanne stared at the bag in her hands, then up at her trusted woman. "How did you manage that?"

Beatrice blushed slightly. "The stable boy is sweet on me, and has agreed to help get you off the premises, but you must go, now!"

"Where in Hades is that betrayer of all that is holy?"

The roared question echoed down the hall and through the door to her chambers, sending a chill through Joanne's body. She had never heard such rage in her husband's voice before, even during the arguments husbands and wives were expected to have after so many years of marriage.

It terrified her.

Beatrice grabbed her by the arm and hauled her toward the door leading to the servants' passageway. "There's no more time."

Joanne no longer resisted, her husband's tirade continuing, there no doubt he meant her harm.

And she wouldn't blame him.

If the accusations were true.

She scurried down the narrow hallway with Beatrice in the lead, her heart hammering, tears flowing down her cheeks as she tried not to faint from the terror she now felt.

A thought occurred to her, nearly bringing her to a halt. "Where will I go?"

But Beatrice had thought of everything. "To your cousin's."

"My cousin?"

"Yes, Sir Henri, remember? He married and has a farm in Crécy-la-Chapelle."

Joanne placed the name after a moment, then her face paled. "But I barely know him! I haven't seen him in years!"

6

"He's family, and the fact he is almost forgotten is exactly why you must go to him. No one will think to look for you there. I will send word when it's safe."

They emerged from the hallway to the outside, Albert, the stable boy, waiting by the door, Joanne's horse at his side. Beatrice hugged her hard. "You be safe, Milady."

"Where is that adulteress that would call herself my wife!"

Joanne paled, as did Beatrice, who shoved her toward the horse. "Go! Now!" she hissed before stepping back inside and closing the door. Albert helped her mount the horse, but she hesitated as she heard Beatrice on the other side of the door respond to her master's question.

"I'm sorry, sir, but I haven't seen her since breakfast."

"You're lying! I'll have the truth from you, even if I have to kill you to get it!"

Joanne gasped as she heard a sharp crack and a cry from Beatrice, the poor girl clearly struck by her irate husband. She moved to dismount, to help the defenseless girl, when Albert reached up and pushed her back into the saddle.

"You mustn't, Milady." He smacked her horse on the hindquarters and it whinnied in protest before racing toward the open gates, the cries of Beatrice echoing in Joanne's head.

Please, Lord, save the poor girl from my husband!

De Rancourt Residence
Crécy-la-Chapelle, Kingdom of France

"I'd rather be in battle, fighting Saracens," grumbled Simon Chastain, Sir Marcus de Rancourt's trusted sergeant and good friend.

Marcus stood and stretched his tired muscles, then regarded his sergeant. "*I'd* rather you be in battle too. At least then you'd be in the Holy Land, which is definitely downwind. Have you smelled yourself lately?"

Simon leaned on the pitchfork he had been piling hay with, and gave his master a look. "Have you yourself? You're no rosebush, my friend."

Marcus took an exaggerated smell of his armpit and genuinely winced. "Have we become smellier, or is it just that we're no longer surrounded by hundreds of men who all smell as bad?"

Simon glanced at the barn, filled with livestock and horses. "I think we've degenerated into animals. Perhaps we should be living with them, rather than in our own quarters." He glanced at the incomplete barracks on the large property. "The facilities *were* much more civilized at our barracks in the Holy Land."

Marcus glanced at the half-built barracks still under construction by the townsfolk in their spare time, the completed barn rebuilt by the guilty feelings of the same men who had burned down the original. It had been the priority, and his men hadn't minded waiting

8

for their own barracks as their new situation was worked out.

Sir Marcus was a Templar Knight, and still was, though given special dispensation by the Grand Master to continue in his role, despite his circumstances. His sister had died, leaving her two children—his niece and nephew—orphaned. He had returned too late, and had reluctantly agreed to take on the responsibility of raising the two young children, saving them from an uncertain life. It had meant giving up his life of soldiering, effectively curtailed regardless by a Saracen arrow not four months earlier, weakening his left shoulder.

His men, Simon, whom he had fought with for over two decades, and his two squires, David and Jeremy, who had been with him for the better part of a decade, had all agreed to stay with him and work the farm he had inherited, his late brother-in-law deceased, having died two years earlier, saving young Angeline from drowning. He had never met the man, but from what he had been told, he had been a loving husband and father, who used his limited means, and distant aristocratic title, to provide his family with a better life than most in these parts.

But without anyone to work the farm, and no one to take care of the children, they would have been left destitute, given to the church, or worse, left to fend for themselves. It was something for which Marcus knew his sister would never have forgiven him, had he let it happen.

He stared at his young nephew Jacques and the orphaned Pierre, his parents murdered several weeks ago, leaving him with no one to care for him. As they brushed the horses, his niece Angeline collected the eggs from their chickens. He smiled at the sight. "We may smell, but we've done a good thing."

The rest of his men stopped what they were doing, following his gaze. Jeremy spoke first. "I have no regrets, sir."

"Nor I," agreed David.

Simon growled. "I have a few, one of which is agreeing to share accommodations with you two."

Marcus chuckled. "You'll each have your own room when the barracks are complete, as I promised."

Jeremy smiled. "I think that will be the first time I've had my own room in my entire life." His eyes bulged. "I think I might get lonely!"

David grinned. "Then find yourself a nice young lass to share your bed with!"

Jeremy rubbed his chin. "*That* is the most intelligent thing I think I've ever heard you say."

"I'm not just a pretty face."

"No, you're definitely not that."

"I said *just*."

"I know what you said. Have you ever actually seen your face? It is quite revolting."

David paused. "You know, I don't know if I ever actually have, come to think of it." He jabbed a finger at Jeremy. "I just hope I'm not as ugly as you are. That would be a sin."

"It would also explain your success with the ladies."

"I've been as successful as you, I assure you!"

10

"I am not ashamed to admit I've had limited success. I take it as a matter of pride that I've been able to resist the temptations of the flesh."

David snorted. "Easy to resist when you have no prospects."

Tanya, the farm's mastiff that had taken a liking to Marcus, the new alpha male of the homestead, growled, her nose pointing down the path leading to the farm. They all turned to see someone on horseback racing toward the property, half a dozen in pursuit several hundred paces behind.

"Is that a woman?" asked Simon, raising a hand to shield his eyes from the sun high in the western sky.

"Help!" cried the person on horseback, waving at them, answering the question.

Marcus bristled. "Weapons!"

The men scrambled toward the barracks as he rushed toward the home where he lived with the children. "Come!" he ordered Tanya, who dutifully followed. The last thing he needed was the eager beast frightening the horse upon which the lady in distress rode. "My sword!" he shouted, and Isabelle Leblanc, the young woman whose family was helping them during this transition period, appeared in the doorway for a moment, her eyes bulging at the approaching sight, before disappearing inside. She reemerged as he reached the doorway, tossing him his sword. He yanked it from its scabbard and raced down the path toward the woman, Tanya at his side, his men emerging from their unfinished quarters, Simon with his sword, David and Jeremy with their bows and arrows.

11

"Help me! You must help me!" cried the woman, dressed far finer than any he had seen in these parts. He reached up and grabbed the horse by the lead, steadying it as she came to a halt, her pursuers pounding nearer. "Is this the de Foix farm?"

Marcus nodded. "It is."

The woman gasped in relief as her shoulders collapsed. "Then you must be my cousin, Sir Henri de Foix. I am Lady Joanne de Rohan. We met some ten years ago at my father's estate. You must help me! I fear they intend to kill me!"

Marcus had no time to decide whether to believe her or not, nor correct her on the mistaken identity. He was *not* her cousin. Henri was his brother-in-law, dead two years. All that did matter was that this was a lady, and if a relation, she was aristocracy, and nothing could justify what now arrived on his property—six men, armed, with no sign of good intentions on their faces. He placed himself between her and the new arrivals as Simon joined him at his side, David and Jeremy taking up flanking positions to his left and right, a good hundred paces off.

"Identify yourself!"

One of their uninvited guests advanced. "I am Louis Forbin, captain of Lord Charles de Rohan's guard."

"And by what right do you intrude upon my property?" demanded Marcus, his sword casually over his shoulder as the men appeared content to remain upon their horses, but not on the attack.

"By right of this woman's husband, Lord Charles. We are here to arrest her."

Marcus concealed his surprise. "On what charge?"

"Adultery."

This time Marcus failed as his eyebrows rose slightly.

Adultery?

He glanced back at the woman, vehemently shaking her head.

"I swear to you, I am innocent of these charges. I have never been unfaithful to my husband, in body or in spirit."

Marcus turned back toward the men. "The lady claims she is innocent. What evidence do you have of her guilt?"

Captain Forbin sneered. "I require none. I have orders from my master to bring her back to Paris so she can be arrested, and I intend to fulfill my duty."

Marcus tapped the hilt of his sword. "Do you know who I am?"

"It is of no concern of mine."

"I am *Sir* Marcus de Rancourt, Templar Knight, and sworn to protect the innocent. This is my sergeant"—Simon bowed slightly—"and my squires. We have decades of experience fighting the Saracen. I suggest if you intend to press the matter, you leave now and return with more men so that it can at least be a fair fight."

Forbin drew his sword, quickly followed by the rest. "You'll find I have little time for Templars."

Marcus smiled. "Prepare to make the time."

The man's horse reared up on its hind legs then leaped forward, followed by the others. Marcus took a step back, preparing himself as an arrow embedded itself in the thigh of Forbin, another in the shoulder of the man to his right. Both cried out as they slumped forward, their momentum killed as their rides sought instructions no longer provided. Marcus surged forward, reaching up and grabbing Forbin by the arm and hauling him off his horse, booting him in the head as he hit the ground. Tanya lunged forward and Marcus pointed at the downed captain.

"Stay!"

Tanya stopped, growling at the man, but holding her position. A grunt on the other side of Forbin's horse indicated Simon had taken his man down as the thuds of two more arrows finding their marks were heard, two more cries confirming success.

Marcus raised his left arm. "Halt!" he ordered, pressing the tip of his blade against the captain's throat. "End this now, or he dies, then so do you!"

Those still on their horses stopped, uncertain of what to do, their swords slowly lowering as David and Jeremy closed the gap, ensuring their arrows would penetrate the chainmail even deeper should they loose them.

"Drop your swords."

Swords clattered to the ground, and Marcus lifted his foot off the captain's chest. "Tend to your wounded, and be off with you."

The two uninjured men dismounted and helped their wounded comrades back onto their horses. Marcus grabbed the lead of Forbin's horse, staring up at him. "Take this message to your master. I will be coming to Paris to find out the truth in this matter. He has my word as a Templar that should I be shown sufficient proof that she is indeed guilty, I will hand her over to the Court myself. Understood?"

14

Forbin nodded, and Marcus released his horse, the man flicking the reins and heading back down the path with the others. He paused, turning back slightly. "Templar Knight, I would say something to you."

Marcus crossed his arms. "Proceed."

"You know not what you have done here, this day. I fear you will not live to regret it."

"Is that a threat?"

David and Jeremy stretched their bows.

"No, it is merely a warning. You have become involved in something far more dangerous than you can possibly imagine, and one lone knight will not be able to stop what has already begun."

Marcus smiled. "Fortunately, I am not alone."

Simon growled beside him, Tanya joining in. Forbin turned again, leading his failed band off the farm. Marcus watched until they were out of sight, then motioned toward Jeremy. "Make sure they leave town."

"Yes, sir." Jeremy sprinted for the barn to retrieve a horse as Marcus turned his attention to their new arrival.

"I'm sorry, Milady, but what was your name again?"

"I am Lady Joanne de Rohan, your cousin on your mother's side. Third cousin, I believe."

Marcus bowed slightly. "I am Sir Marcus de Rancourt, and I regret to inform you that I am not your cousin. Sir Henri, sadly, died two years ago after saving his daughter from drowning."

Her shoulders slumped as Isabelle raced from the house, Angeline, Jacques, and Pierre remaining in the doorway, their tear-stained cheeks revealing they had seen too much of what had just happened.

"What is going on here?" demanded Isabelle.

Marcus shrugged. "I'm not entirely certain. This is Lady Joanne de Rohan, cousin to my late brother-in-law, Henri."

Lady Joanne's face brightened as she stared at him. "Then we *are* related, through marriage!"

Marcus grunted. "I suppose we are."

"Then you must help me!" She stared at Isabelle. "Are you my cousin's wife?"

Isabelle laughed. "He should be so lucky!" She motioned toward the children. "Two of these are your cousin's children. I'm merely helping out around here until these *men* can learn to take care of themselves." She gave Marcus a scowl, the others grinning, Marcus not entirely convinced they were correct in their belief she secretly harbored feelings toward him, her displays of hatred the proof. "Come, let's get you inside and settled, then you can tell us what is going on."

Marcus had to admit having Isabelle around was convenient. She was an excellent cook, took care of their domestic needs—though through bitter complaints of neglecting her own chores at her home—and was remarkably efficient and wise in handling the unexpected.

Like today.

Marcus would have merely grilled the new arrival for answers, though Isabelle's method would probably prove more effective. He watched as the two disappeared inside, Jeremy returning.

"They stopped outside of town to tend to their wounds, but I overheard the captain say they would return to Paris for instructions."

"Good." He gestured toward the barn. "I'll be heading in the same direction. Prepare my horse for the journey."

"Yes, sir."

Simon held out a hand, halting Jeremy. "Sir, you shouldn't go alone."

"I can't leave the women alone, not if these men intend to return."

David stepped forward. "Sir, Jeremy and I can manage. You should take Simon with you. You'll need someone to watch your back."

Marcus stared at David. "I suppose you're right."

"I usually am." David bowed deeply. "With all due respect, of course."

Marcus chuckled. "Very well. Prepare both our horses." He headed toward the house. "Let's find out what is really going on, shall we?"

Crécy-la-Chapelle, Kingdom of France

Isabelle Leblanc served the clearly terrified woman a *tisane*, a pot of which she always had at the ready, a habit her mother had ingrained in her since her earliest memories. She wasn't sure why she was still here, taking care of these foolish men, neglecting her duties to her family and her aging mother. She kept telling herself it was for the children, and it was, but she knew, deep down, it was really Sir Marcus that kept her here.

And it was heartbreaking, because nothing could ever come of it.

A Templar Knight, sworn to celibacy, could never take a wife, not while still a member of the Order. His men, any of whom would make a reasonable mate in these parts, were intensely loyal to him, and she doubted would ever leave his side, even with all she had to offer a man.

Yet none of them interested her.

It's hopeless.

She served the tisane with a smile, and the woman took a sip with shaking hands, closing her eyes as she tried to regain control. "Don't you worry, Milady, Sir Marcus is a good man and will take care of everything, I'm sure."

Lady Joanne smiled weakly. "I-I hope so. I was hoping to find my cousin. Family, you understand."

Isabelle patted Joanne's hand. "While your cousin's death was a tragedy, in these circumstances, I think Sir Marcus will be better able to assist you. He is a rather

18

remarkable man, with the resources of the Templars behind him."

Joanne took another sip of her drink, then nodded. "Perhaps you're right." She looked up as Marcus and Simon entered.

"They're gone, at least for now." Marcus took a seat at the table, Simon standing watch at the door. "Now, Lady Joanne, why don't you tell me everything, from the beginning."

The woman put her cup down, her hand still shaking. "It-it all happened so suddenly, there isn't much to tell. A letter was delivered to our home this morning, from whom, I do not know. The letter was presented to my chambermaid who was to take it to my husband. The seal had cracked, so her curiosity won out. She read the letter on her way to deliver it, and immediately realized the danger it posed."

Marcus interrupted her. "Your chambermaid can read?"

Joanne nodded. "Yes, I've been teaching her for years. Something to occupy my time, as we have no children."

"I understand. Please, continue."

"Well, she knew she had to deliver it, otherwise she may get in serious trouble, but instead of delivering it into my husband's hands, she placed it under the tray used to serve his morning meal."

Isabelle nodded in appreciation. "Clever girl."

Joanne agreed. "Yes, and faithful to a fault."

Marcus shifted in his chair. "And what did this letter say?"

"I'm not sure exactly what was said, my girl only giving me the highlights to make me understand the urgency, but in summary, it accused me of committing adultery with another man, that there were witnesses, and proof would be forthcoming."

Simon grunted, avoiding eye contact. "And you…"

"I'm innocent, of course."

Simon bowed. "Of course."

Marcus dismissed the question with the flick of his wrist. "Of course you are, Milady. How did you make your escape?"

"Well, my girl warned me, and while I debated what to do, she arranged a horse and provisions with the stable boy. She returned, my husband having since found the letter, and compelled me to leave rather than discuss the matter with him. I dare say she was correct to force me to leave, as I fear I'd be in a dungeon now if it weren't for her. She remembered my cousin living here, and I made my way. Obviously, he must have forced my girl to talk, as he wouldn't have known where to find me. He sent men after me, who caught up with me just as I reached this town." She paled slightly and clasped a hand to her chest. "Oh no, I hope Beatrice is all right!"

Marcus didn't say anything, but if he was thinking what Isabelle was, it couldn't have been good. A woman as loyal to her mistress as Beatrice sounded, would have only given up what she knew through torture or threat of death.

"Did your girl say who you supposedly had this affair with?" asked Marcus.

Joanne shook her head. "No, though like I said, she only gave me a brief description of what the letter contained."

Marcus rose, Simon immediately straightening. "Milady—Cousin, you will remain here with two of my trusted men. My sergeant and I will travel to Paris immediately, and meet with your husband. Hopefully, we'll be able to find out the truth behind this, before it is too late."

Tears poured from Joanne's eyes as she clasped her hands to her chest. "Oh, thank you, Cousin, thank you! Your mistress here was right. You *are* a good man."

Marcus glanced at Isabelle, her eyes quickly darting to the floor as her cheeks flushed. "I hesitate to ask—"

Isabelle steeled herself then glared at him, throwing her hands up in the air. "Of course, of course. I'll help watch the children, and take care of your cousin."

Marcus bowed. "I appreciate your sacrifice."

Isabelle was about to snap an annoyed response when she spotted Simon grinning at her. "And what has you all smiles?"

Simon stared at his feet. "Umm, nothing." He beat a hasty retreat out the door and Marcus chuckled.

"Cousin, I'll get you to write down for me your husband's name, how to get to your home, and the name of your chambermaid. I shall look out for her personally."

Isabelle grabbed a quill and paper, placing it in front of their guest. Marcus stepped toward the doorway, watching as his squires brought two fresh horses from the stables, provisioned for the short journey to Paris. She found her eyes roaming his body, imagining what magnificence was hidden by the soiled clothes he now wore from his toils in the field.

I wonder what it looks like.

She had never seen one. She had never been with a man. She had kissed a boy when she was barely ten, though it was an innocent, experimental thing that was at once exciting and disgusting.

But with Marcus?

She had dreamed of kissing him from the moment she had first laid eyes upon him. If there were someone in this world to lose her precious gift to, it was this man standing in front of her. But her infatuation went far beyond their first meeting less than a month ago. It ran back years. Marcus was twice her age, if not more, and it was his sister Nicoline that had spoken of him for years, since she had first found herself expressing any interest in boys. He was always described in such idealistic terms, she had built up an image of him in her mind that she had fallen in love with. When she had finally met him, he had been such a disappointment in some ways that it had angered her, until she finally realized that her only real disappointment was that he hadn't immediately declared his own love for her, and they weren't already planning their wedding.

It wasn't his fault. He was a celibate Templar, and she was merely a young woman in his eyes, something to be tolerated more than anything else. She had little doubt that once one of his men took on a wife, they would continue to live at the farm and this new addition would replace her, relegating her back to her own home. She would have to take a husband soon, and God knew there were enough suitors in the village that would have her, but she didn't want them.

She wanted Marcus.

And she could never have him.

"Here's everything I can think of that you might need."

Marcus turned, catching Isabelle's stare before she had a chance to turn away. He took the paper from Joanne and quickly read it. "Excellent. My squires, David and Jeremy, will remain here with you. Hopefully I will return with good news within a couple of days."

Joanne frowned. "And should you not?"

"Milady, I must confess that I made a commitment to uphold justice, no matter what that might be. If I find that you have lied to me, then, relation or not, I will hand you over to the authorities."

"Sir Marcus!" cried Isabelle, her eyes flaring as she spun on him. "How could you say such a thing!"

Marcus raised a finger, silencing her. "But I will also say this. I believe you, Milady, and I will do everything in my power to find out the truth, and bring to justice those who would do you harm."

De Rohan Residence
Paris, Kingdom of France

"Did you notice they only had one guard on the gate?"

Sir Marcus glanced at his sergeant as they waited for his cousin's husband, Lord Charles de Rohan, to meet with them. "Perhaps it's because we took out four of their men."

Simon chuckled. "Perhaps."

"And this is Paris, after all. If one can't be safe here, where can one?"

Simon grunted. "True, I suppose. I guess I'm just used to the Holy Land where a Saracen blade awaits you at every turn."

Marcus sighed. "I do miss it."

Simon laughed. "I as well. Though farming has its perks."

Marcus' eyebrows rose and he turned toward his friend. "Oh?"

"Yes. I can't think of a single one at the moment, but I'm sure it does."

Marcus smiled, turning toward the footsteps coming down the hall. "I'm sure you'll think of one at some point." He smiled and bowed as the lord of the manor entered. "Lord Charles, I am Sir Marcus de Rancourt, and this is my sergeant, Simon Chastain. Thank you for agreeing to meet with us."

The man eyed Marcus from head to toe, no doubt the Templar surcoat giving him pause, and probably the only reason they had been permitted an audience without an explanation. "Of course. What business do you have with me?"

"It concerns your wife, Lady Joanne."

Charles' eyes widened. "My wife? What of her?"

"She came to me earlier today, seeking protection from men under your employ. Apparently, she is accused of adultery."

Charles' eyes flared and his cheeks reddened. "The woman is *not* accused, she is guilty!"

"She swears she is innocent."

Charles waved his hand, dismissing the words. "I know her to be a liar. The letter was clear. I know the man she is accused of being involved with, and he has no honor or shame, and I have been assured there are witnesses, and proof will be forthcoming. If she were innocent, why would I have received such a letter?"

Marcus bowed slightly. "If everything in the letter were true, I would agree, but I have spoken to your wife, and I find her to be sincere. I believe in order for justice to be served, we must determine the truth."

"I know the truth!"

"Based upon facts that may be in dispute." Marcus raised a hand slightly, cutting off the tirade about to erupt from their host. "I propose this. I am a Templar, and my word is my bond. I will find out the truth, whatever it may be, and once I know what is happening, I will inform you first."

The man paused, staring at Marcus. He pursed his lips then drew a deep breath. "Even if that truth reveals my wife *is* an adulteress?"

"Yes. And in exchange, you promise to leave your wife alone until the truth is discovered. Agreed?"

Charles paced for a moment, scratching his chin, then spun toward Marcus. "Agreed."

Marcus smiled. "Thank you, sir. Now, may I ask, who is she accused of having an affair with?"

"Sir Denys de Montfort. The man is a member of the King's Court, and a constant thorn in too many sides. He's exactly the sort to conduct such an unholy undertaking. A constant womanizer, in my opinion."

"And where may we find him?"

"His home is not far from here. I will give you directions."

"Very well. One more thing."

Charles exhaled loudly. "What?"

"Your wife's chambermaid, Beatrice. What have you done to her?"

Charles' eyebrows rose. "She is locked in her room, under guard until I decide her fate."

"Did you lay hands on her?"

"None more than was necessary to gain the truth."

Marcus frowned, leaning slightly closer to Charles. "I will trust you not to molest her any further until we determine what has taken place here today." Marcus detected a slight tremble in Charles' lip.

"You have my word."

26

De Montfort Residence
Paris, Kingdom of France

"That is no one's business but my own and Lady Joanne's."

Marcus regarded Sir Denys de Montfort. He was a handsome man, at least in Marcus' inexpert opinion. Young, perhaps mid-twenties, and easily a decade junior to Lady Joanne. Marcus found him slightly arrogant in their brief interaction so far, as if he were above the consequences of such accusations.

"Are you aware that Lord Charles knows of your transgressions, and is demanding satisfaction?"

Sir Denys shrugged, dismissing the question with a wave of his hand. "Why should I care what that imbecile wants? Let him produce his proof if it exists."

"Lady Joanne claims she is innocent, and that no such affair has taken place."

Denys paused, his jaw sagging slightly. He grunted. "Nonsense. If that were true, it was merely to protect me. She loves me, and we have been, shall we say, intimate. There is no denying her feelings."

Marcus splayed his hands. "I can only tell you what she herself has told me. She claims to have never been unfaithful, in mind or body, and that this entire notion of her having an affair is false. And, frankly, I believe her."

Denys tossed his head back and laughed. "And what would you know of love, a Templar Knight who is sworn to celibacy, and has probably never bedded a woman, let alone felt the love and joy in one's heart at having met the one woman in the world who can truly make you glad to be alive."

Marcus bowed slightly. "I will concede that you understand the affairs of the flesh and heart far better than I ever will, however, you are aware that you could face serious consequences if you are found guilty of such an affair?"

Denys' smile slowly dissipated. "Yes, I am aware of this, and it weighs heavily on my heart. We have kept our affair in strict confidence, yet should word come out, there is little I can do except embrace it."

"Despite what it will do to Lady Joanne, who proclaims her innocence? Wouldn't it be better for her if you would simply back up her story and also claim there had been no affair? That this letter is false?"

"But didn't you state that the letter claimed there were witnesses and that proof would follow? Surely once what has been promised is produced, there will be no denying it by her or myself. And should that occur, wouldn't it be better to declare our love for each other, rather than let those of the Court believe it was merely some tawdry affair of the flesh?"

Marcus sighed. The man was right in everything he said, though he feared the consequences would ultimately be the same. The King's Court would care nothing of why the affair had taken place, merely that it had. Lady Joanne would be imprisoned, and Sir Denys perhaps put to death.

It was yet another reason he was happy to have taken the vow of celibacy decades ago.

The affairs of the heart too often led to sin.

"I doubt they will be swayed by your commitment to each other, Sir Denys."

Denys frowned at him then quickly headed from the room. "Come with me, I would show you something."

Marcus exchanged a look with Simon, who had stood silently to the side the entire time, mostly shaking his head in disbelief. They followed the proud adulterer down a hall then into a large room, well lit by lamps and a roaring fire.

Denys motioned toward a large portrait showing him standing along the River Seine, a woman at his side, staring up at him lovingly, her hand on his chest. "Is this not proof of my love?"

Marcus stared at the large painting, the quality exceptional, the likeness of Denys striking, and the woman at his side equally beautiful. "I'm sorry, I don't understand."

"I had it commissioned from an artist I have been patron to for several years now. Lady Joanne has no idea I've had it made. My friend met her on two occasions, and was able to sketch her surreptitiously without her knowing, then used those sketches to create this incredible likeness. I intend to give it to her tonight when we meet, as a gift, a declaration of my love for her."

Marcus approached the painting, staring at the woman. "Do you consider this a good likeness?"

"As if she were in the room with me now."

"Are you sure?"

"Absolutely. She is as accurate as I."

Marcus nodded slowly, staring at Denys then the painting, the resemblance between him and the

29

likeness in the portrait remarkably accurate, the artist undoubtedly a talent. He beckoned Simon who stared at it as well for a moment, then shook his head. Marcus turned to Denys. "I'm not sure how to say this, Sir Denys, but this isn't Lady Joanne."

Denys stared at him in stunned silence for a moment. "What do you mean?"

"I mean, I met her today, and this is *not* my cousin."

Denys' laughed. "Then whomever you met is an imposter."

Marcus sighed. "Sir, I think someone is an imposter here, but I doubt it is the woman I met. I can see no possible reason for a woman to seek me out, claim to be someone she is not, and deny an affair that the real Lady Joanne was having."

Denys' shoulders sagged slightly, most of the pride in his posture now gone, confusion on his face. "You're right, of course. That *does* make little sense."

Marcus lowered his voice, taking on a more gentle tone. "I think, sir, something more is going on here than either of us realizes."

Denys collapsed into a nearby chair. "I-I agree. But why? What did—?" He threw his arms against the sides of the chair. "I'm so confused!"

"Yes, sir, as am I, but we must find out the truth. My cousin's life is at stake, as is her marriage, the honor of her husband, and frankly, sir, your life as well."

Denys' mouth widened. "Why, you're right! If what you say is true, and this woman isn't Lady Joanne, then I am being accused of a crime I only *thought* I was committing, not one I have actually committed. I could die for nothing!"

Marcus ignored the selfishness of the declaration. "You said you were going to give her the portrait tonight. Does that mean you had plans to meet her?"

"Yes. I'm supposed to see her shortly."

"Then I suggest you keep that meeting."

Denys leaped to his feet, color returning to his cheeks as rage blazed in his eyes. "I agree! I will get the truth out of her, for sure!"

Marcus shook his head, waving his hands. "No, let us do that. You will meet with her, pretend all is well, then we will take her into our custody, and determine what she is playing at."

Rue St. Denis
Paris, Kingdom of France

"If that fool doesn't calm down, he'll give himself away."

Marcus nodded at Simon's observation. Sir Denys was pacing impatiently back and forth beside his carriage, his rapid, angry turns certainly not those of a man eager to meet with his illicit lover. "It's too late now. We can't risk going and telling him to settle down. We'll just have to pray that when she does appear, he can maintain control, at least for a few moments."

Simon grunted. "I can't believe we are trying to catch a woman having an affair. How far we've fallen."

Marcus chuckled. "I agree I never would have pictured us in such a situation, though I'm disheartened to hear you feel it's a fall."

Simon sighed. "Perhaps I chose my words poorly. It's just I thought I would die with my brothers, fighting the enemies of God, not trying to determine who is sleeping with whom, in the back alleys of Paris."

Marcus stifled an outright laugh. "I share your feelings, I assure you. But think of it this way. What did we swear to do? We swore to fight for our Lord Jesus Christ, and defend His ministry. What more honorable task is there than trying to protect an innocent woman, who has done nothing wrong, from a horrible fate? We've already determined that she is

32

most likely innocent, and now we have a chance to prove it, and quite possibly save her life."

Simon nodded. "Well, when you put it that way, I feel like a heel."

"Speaking of ungodly smells."

Simon leaned in and sniffed. "Good thing we both had baths before we left, otherwise we might never have gained entry into such lofty estates."

"It was a good thought of Isabelle's."

"I think she was simply hoping for a look at your attractive calves."

Marcus shook his head. "Are we back to this? That woman does *not* like me, and even if she did, there's nothing that could come of it."

"You haven't thought of leaving the Order, now that we can no longer serve it as we had before?"

"Not for a moment. You?"

"I serve at your side."

Marcus turned to him. "And were I to die?"

Simon frowned. "I'm not sure. I suppose I could return to the Holy Land to die on the battlefield, though with each passing year, I turn more into a liability than an asset." He looked at Marcus. "Are you planning on dying soon?"

Marcus eyed him. "If I survive this conversation, then no."

Simon shrugged. "You're making it difficult to make future plans. *That* being said, should something happen to you, those children will still need a provider, and I would consider it my duty to fulfill that role."

33

Marcus smiled. "You're a good man, Simon Chastain. A very good man."

"I am a saint. But I make no promises that should you pass, I won't renounce my vow of celibacy, and win the heart of the beautiful Isabelle."

Marcus chuckled. "And you would have my blessing, my good friend, though I have a feeling she might put up quite the fight. Have you seen yourself? Your face is scarred like a desert oasis gone dry."

Simon rubbed a hand over his face. "It adds character, does it not?"

"It adds something." Marcus held up a hand. "Wait, I see someone."

He peered into the darkness, the only light from the full moon. A shadow moved quickly toward the carriage, and Denys spun to meet it. The figure, slight enough to be a woman, stretched out her arms and grabbed her lover, Denys thankfully staying in character and returning the embrace. Words were exchanged, unheard from their position, but with Denys now holding her, Marcus strode quickly forward, followed by Simon, who kept to the shadows to take up a position behind her.

The woman spotted Marcus and she gasped, pulling away from Denys, who held her tightly as she struggled against him. Marcus held up a hand.

"Milady, there really is no point in trying to run." He motioned behind her at Simon, now in position. "You cannot get away."

"What is this? What is the meaning of this?" She stared up at Denys. "Please, my love, what are you doing?"

34

"You dare call me that, after everything you have done?"

Her jaw dropped. "I don't understand? What do you mean? You know I love you, with all my heart! Do you-do you not love me any longer?"

She seemed genuinely distressed, and if she were not the Lady Joanne, she was playing her part exceptionally well. Well enough that Marcus had a twinge of doubt. Could the woman on his farm be the imposter, and not this one? She matched the portrait exactly, the artist having proven his skill, and the woman was dressed as he would expect a lady of fine standing to be, even her hair and carriage unquestionably proper.

He decided to ask the question directly. "You claim to be Lady Joanne?"

"Claim? What kind of question is that? Of course I'm Lady Joanne. Now please, explain to me what is going on here! This is an outrage!"

Marcus folded his arms. "Today I met my cousin, Lady Joanne. She was *not* you."

"Then you met a liar." She tore herself away from Denys, though remained standing in front of his carriage. "I find your questions offensive, and this treatment unacceptable and undignified. I demand you let me go so I can return to my husband. Clearly this was a mistake, and I wish this entire business to end." A tear rolled down her cheek, her reactions still precisely as he would expect.

"So, you still claim to be Lady Joanne?"

"Of course I do."

Marcus sighed. "Very well. Then I can see only one way to settle the matter."

De Rohan Residence
Paris, Kingdom of France

Lord Charles de Rohan entered the room they had been shown to, his robes and disheveled appearance suggesting he had been asleep some time, and was not pleased at having been woken. It was probably wise that Marcus had insisted Sir Denys return to his residence.

Charles might have run him through on sight.

"What business do you have that requires you to wake me at such an hour?"

Marcus bowed, as did Simon. "I apologize, sir, but I was confident you would want to hear what we have discovered."

Charles stared at him for a moment, then at their female companion. "Who is this?"

"She claims to be your wife, sir."

Charles laughed. "Ridiculous! She doesn't look at all like my wife. This is but a child." He drew a dagger from under his robes and pressed it against the woman's neck before Marcus could stop him. "Tell me why you have done this, now, and I may let you live."

The woman glared at him defiantly, though as the dagger pressed harder against her throat, her will broke and her shoulders slumped. "Oh, what's the point now?"

Marcus exchanged a surprised look with Simon, the woman's voice changing from that of a lady, to one of the lower classes, her entire demeanor different. It even surprised Charles, as he stepped back, withdrawing his blade.

Marcus put himself between the two to prevent any other such altercation. "What is your real name?"

"Melanie Girard."

"Very well, Miss Girard, please explain yourself."

"I was paid to pretend to be her, you know. A bit of a lark, I guess."

"Paid by whom?"

"I don't know. It was good money, though, and he never treated me poorly. I thought it was some sort of prank, you know, that eventually he'd reveal the truth to Denys, but it kept getting more serious, and before I knew it, we were, you know, biblical."

Charles dropped into a seat. "But why? Why impersonate my wife?"

She shrugged, dropping into another seat, her knees spread wide. "I dunno. It's really too bad. I actually like Denys. *Really* like him. He's really sweet, and I know he loves me, but, well, it's not really me, is it? He'd probably shove me aside if I approached him on the street."

Marcus was still shocked at the complete transformation before him. "And he had no idea you weren't actually Lady Joanne?"

"None. I desperately wanted to tell him the truth, but, well, I feared it would end the relationship, and it was nice to experience how royalty lives. But if I told him, he'd likely have me arrested, and I'd lose both him and the money the gentleman was paying me to play my part."

Marcus held out a hand, silencing the question about to erupt from Charles' mouth. "This gentleman, who was he?"

She shrugged. "I don't know. I never saw his face and he disguises his voice. I tried to see it the first time I met him in a public place, but he wore a hood that hid his features. All I know is that since that first meeting, I meet with him after I see Denys, to tell him what happened. A few days later, I'll receive a message with new instructions and payment for my services."

"When do you see him next?"

"I'm supposed to see him tonight, after my date with Denys."

Marcus drew a quick breath of excitement. "When?"

"Midnight."

"Then we still have time."

Rue St. Denis
Paris, Kingdom of France

"This is an odd affair."

Marcus nodded at Simon as they followed Miss Girard in her carriage, met at the appointed hour as if she had kept her illicit meeting with Sir Denys. "It is indeed. This intrigue with women is yet another reason I prefer life in the Order than as a common man."

"Agreed. A few moments of infrequent pleasure are not worth the difficulties a woman can introduce into one's life."

Marcus pursed his lips. "And yet, for time immemorial, men have made the same mistake repeatedly. There must be something we're missing."

"We *are* the wrong two men to be debating the pros and cons of men and women associating with each other."

Marcus chuckled. "You are right, there. Alas, we'll never know, my friend. I prefer the love of my brothers and the Lord, than that of any woman's heart."

"It is a difficult life we have chosen for ourselves."

"It is, but the rewards will be boundless in the next life."

"Amen. If they're not, I'm seeking out Hugues de Payens and those other scoundrels who founded the Order, and kicking their asses."

Marcus stifled a belly laugh, reminding himself they were on a clandestine mission, the carriage in the not too far distance carrying their imposter to meet the man who had hired her. They hoped to capture him at the prearranged meeting, though he was concerned for the girl's safety—if her employer had been observing from a distance, he would have seen their altercation of several hours ago.

"They're stopping."

Marcus slowed, his unfamiliarity with the city a distinct disadvantage. It had barely been three weeks since they had arrived from the Holy Land in response to his sister's desperate letter, a letter that had arrived too late. It had meant a drastic change to all their lives, and though he had to admit he was enjoying life with the children, it was little diversions such as today's that kept him on his toes.

Marcus shifted his horse deeper into the shadows as Miss Girard stepped out of the carriage, looking both ways as if searching for her benefactor.

She cried out and collapsed in a heap.

Simon cursed and Marcus urged his horse into a gallop, swiftly closing the distance between them. He leaped to the ground and rushed to her side as Simon continued forward, blocking the carriage from leaving should the coachman panic.

Marcus grimaced at the arrow piercing the young woman's chest, blood rapidly staining her cream-colored dress as she gasped for breath. She reached up and grabbed his shoulder.

"Please, tell Denys that I'm sorry for what I've done, and that I truly did love him."

Marcus clasped his hand around hers. "You'll tell him yourself."

She smiled then sighed her last breath, making a liar of him.

Horse's hooves pounding on cobblestone drew his attention, no one with nothing to hide having reason to move at such a pace at this time of night. He jumped on his horse and pointed at Simon. "Stay with her!" He urged his horse forward, after whom he was certain was not only the man behind everything, but also the murderer of this simple woman who had been used, for what purpose he did not know.

He rounded a turn in the dark street and spotted a rider ahead, racing along the side of the River Seine, toward a bridge leading to the other side and far better parts of the massive city. He was gaining on the man, his horse clearly the better, and he was brimming with confidence that he would soon catch him, when his adversary approached the bridge. A yell rang out, and moments later Marcus' heart sank as the drawbridge began to rise, the rider leaping over the gap now making its presence known.

Marcus urged his horse onward, even faster than before, determined to make the jump himself, but it was a fruitless effort.

He wasn't going to make it.

He slowed up and watched in anger and dismay as the rider, now safely on the other side of the river, rode off into the darkness, a free man.

As he stared into the fog blanketing the area, focusing on his bad luck, and his adversary's exceptional good fortune, he finally realized something was wrong.

41

There's no boat!

He urged his horse toward the small gatehouse and dismounted. He rapped three times on the flimsy door, and when there was no answer, he kicked it open and stepped inside. A startled man leaped from his chair, raising his hands as he backed away from the controls that operated the bridge.

"Why did you raise the bridge?"

The man paled in the candlelight. "I-I thought there was a boat."

Marcus drew his dagger and flipped it several times in his hand, all the while eying the man. "I beg your pardon?"

"I-I thought I heard a boat."

"I thought that's what you said." Marcus stepped closer and pressed the tip of the blade against the man's chest, hard enough that were it not for the man's soiled shirt, he'd draw blood. "I suggest you tell me the truth, otherwise I'll be forced to cut your heart out."

"He paid me! He said if he were to be crossing at a gallop, he'd yell to me and I was to raise the bridge immediately!"

Marcus pressed a little harder. "And who is he?"

"I-I don't know, I swear! He wore a hood every time we met. I never saw his face."

"When did he pay you?"

"This evening, maybe four hours ago."

"And was this the first time?"

"No, he's been paying me once a week for several months now, but this was the first time he was ever in need of my services."

42

Marcus stepped back, the man speaking freely now. "Is there anything else you can tell me?"

The gatekeeper shrugged, relaxing slightly. "Nothing I can think of. He's a man whose face I've never seen, and who was always dressed in a dark robe with a hood that covered his features."

"Was he tall?"

"Yes, about your height I would say."

"Fat? Thin?"

"Healthy like yourself."

"Beard?"

"Yes, neatly trimmed."

Marcus smiled. "But I thought you said you never saw his face?"

The man's eyes bulged. "I must have! I know he definitely had a beard. Now that I think of it, I have a distinct impression of his chin." He sighed. "But it's the eyes and nose that really make a man. Those, I am positive, I never saw."

Somebody rapped on the door, throwing it open. "Lower the bridge, you fool!"

Marcus turned to face the man, and the impatient arrival stepped back several paces at the sight of the Templar surcoat.

"I'm sorry, sir, I didn't realize."

Marcus bowed slightly. "There's nothing to apologize for. My business here is done." He turned back to the gatekeeper. "Should you remember anything of relevance, relay it to Lord Charles de Rohan. He will know how to reach me."

The gatekeeper shook out a nod then went to work lowering the bridge as Marcus stepped outside.

"You're a friend of Lord Charles?" asked the man now atop his horse, waiting for the bridge.

Marcus shook his head. "No."

"A good thing. Perhaps you have not heard that his wife ran off on him. I've heard rumors of the most dastardly sort."

"One shouldn't believe everything one hears."

"Of course not, but should they prove true, his days in the Court are numbered. A man who cannot control his wife, can hardly be trusted to advise the King in the affairs of state."

De Rohan Residence
Paris, Kingdom of France

Sir Denys paced back and forth in front of the fire, warming the bones chilled by the brisk ride into the den of the lion threatening to end his time on this earth. It was a foolish impulse to come here, yet he had to. This matter was out of control, and though it turned out he had never known Lady Joanne, the woman was innocent, and her husband had to know.

The door opened and the man himself finally entered, his face red with rage at the sight of him. Denys placed a chair between them both. "Lord Charles, I apologize for the late hour, however I felt our business couldn't wait until the morning."

Charles' eyes flared. "You would dare show yourself in my own home, after what you have done!"

Denys raised a calming hand. "Now, apparently you haven't heard. The woman that I thought was your wife, wasn't. Nothing ever happened with Lady Joanne."

"So I have been informed, yet it does not change the fact that you would have bedded another man's wife if it weren't for the deception." He stabbed at the air between them with a finger. "You, sir, have no honor!"

Denys bowed his head slightly in shame, the man right. "In my defense, I was beguiled, told everything I had ever wanted to hear, and how she was in a loveless marriage with no physical intimacy. I thought I was rescuing a woman from a pitiable existence from a man who couldn't care less whether she was in his life or not."

Charles was crimson. "I don't believe that for an instant. You thought you had found a way to embarrass me in front of the Court through my wife. And you would have succeeded if it were not for those Templars who have uncovered the truth!"

Denys felt a flash of anger at the accusation his motives were political. "You fool! She came to me! I was as much a victim here as you!"

Charles snorted. "For you to think such a thing, shows you should never sit in the Court!"

Denys sighed, realizing he had chosen his words poorly. "My heart has been broken, sir."

"Better your heart than my reputation."

There was a knock at the door, and Charles glanced over his shoulder. "Yes?"

A servant entered with a tray, a folded message on it. "From the King's Court, sir. The messenger arrived just moments ago."

Denys' eyes narrowed, never having received a message from the court at this hour himself. He watched as Charles read it, his eyes widening with each word. He handed it to Denys.

"What is it?" he asked as he answered his own question, quickly reading the shocking message.

His jaw dropped, and Charles glared at him, the rage checked only slightly. "It would appear that I am but one of several whose reputation has been sullied this day."

Denys reread the message before returning it. "This is incredible! It can't be true!"

46

"I hardly think a message would be sent at this hour from the King's Court if it weren't."

Denys shook his head. "But what does it mean?"

"It means we have both been used by someone, and I intend to find out who."

Rue St. Denis
Paris, Kingdom of France

Simon stared into the dark, silently cursing himself for letting Marcus go off on his own. The woman was dead, and a swift blow to the side of the coachman's head would have kept the man out of commission for some time, allowing him to aid his master in the pursuit.

Yet he had his orders.

And he shouldn't worry. Marcus was the greatest warrior he had ever met, his abilities on the battlefield almost legend if admiration were a trait to be sought. But it wasn't. Not for a Templar. Marcus served his Lord as he had sworn to do, and his duty was to protect the Holy Lands and the Christian pilgrims traveling to it, from those who would do them harm.

And he did it exceptionally well.

They all did. A knight with the skills of Marcus was a valuable commodity, and over the decades, he had fought beside those who would become their leaders. It meant small concessions, such as being allowed to keep Simon, Jeremy, and David close.

Simon had served long enough to become a knight himself if he so chose, David and Jeremy long enough to become sergeants.

But none were there for advancement—they were all there to serve their Lord in the best way they could, and all had concluded, on their own, that the way to do that was to ensure Marcus had the best possible men at his side, supporting him.

If something should happen to him...

Simon sighed. He wasn't sure what he would do. He was closer to the man than his own brother, and in fact, wasn't even certain if his own brother was still alive.

Should something happen to his friend, he would keep his word and take care of the children. He smiled slightly at the thought of taking Isabelle as a wife, though the woman would never have him—he was too old and weathered for a young thing like that.

Yet so was Marcus, though he had avoided the leather face that cursed Simon.

The carriage he was leaning against rocked, and he stepped away from it to see the coachman sneak off on the other side. He shook his head then rounded the carriage, approaching the man from the back, grabbing him by the collar.

"And just where do you think you're going?"

The man cringed, squeezing his eyes shut. "I-I want nothing to do with this! I'm just the coachman!"

Simon shoved him to the ground and placed a hand on the hilt of his sword. "What's your name, then?"

"Richard."

"Are you always her coachman?"

Richard nodded, his eyes now opened.

"For how long?"

"Going on two months now, maybe a little longer."

That matches the length of the affair, if Sir Denys is to be believed.

"And who hired you?"

49

"I-I don't know. I was given written orders and a large purse. I was given instructions on where to pick her up the first time, then ever since, before I drop her off, she tells me where and when to pick her up the next time."

"Do you have this letter?"

Richard hesitated, then shook his head. "No. It said to destroy it."

Simon drew his sword several inches from its scabbard. "I'll ask you again. Do you have this letter?"

The man's shoulders slumped, courage begging in this wretched soul. "Yes." He sighed. "The entire situation seemed strange to me, so I thought it best to keep it."

Simon suppressed a smile. "Where is it?"

"Hidden under the floorboards of my room."

"You will take us there when my master returns."

Richard's shoulders slumped further. "Of course."

"What can you tell me about this woman?"

Richard glanced under the carriage at the body on the other side. "Nothing, really. I show up at a certain location at the appointed hour. She climbs in the back, I deliver her to where she says to go, then I wait until she returns. I deliver her to where I picked her up, and she tells me where and when to pick her up the next time."

"And is it always the same place?"

"Yes."

"Every single time?"

Richard opened his mouth to respond, then hesitated. "Actually, once she had me drop her off at a different location. It was raining very heavily, so I don't think she wanted to walk very far."

Simon's heart pounded a little harder. "Where was this?"

"Quai de Gesvres. Not a very good neighborhood, if you ask me, but not much worse than mine, I suppose." He shrugged. "I found it quite odd at the time, though. She dressed as one might expect the aristocracy to, yet she lived in such a place? It made no sense to me."

"Can you take us there?"

Richard frowned. "I get the distinct impression that I have no choice in the matter."

Simon smiled. "I'm glad we understand each other." He spun at the sound of a rider approaching, and sighed with relief at the sight of his master. Marcus swung off his horse and joined them. "Did you catch him?"

Marcus gave him a look. "Do you see him tied to my horse?"

Simon made an exaggerated lean to his left, staring at the horse. "He must have fallen off."

Marcus chuckled then motioned toward the coachman, still on the cold, damp ground. "What's this?"

"Someone tried to make a break for it."

"Sounds like someone with something to hide."

"And you'd be right. He claims to have a letter written by the man who hired him, hidden away in his room. *And,* he claims to have dropped our late friend off at what might be her home."

51

Marcus' eyebrows rose. "And where might that be?"

Simon kicked the man in the foot. "Tell him."

"Quai de Gesvres."

"That sounds as good a place to start as any, but I think we should see this letter first."

Coachman Richard's Residence
Paris, Kingdom of France

Marcus followed the coachman, Richard, up the rickety, narrow stairs hanging to the side of a boarding house that defined poverty. Richard opened the door at the top and they followed him inside. They were greeted with an unlit corridor, any boarders already asleep as it was well past midnight. Richard advanced with confidence, but Marcus held out a hand, silently instructing Simon to leave the door open to let in the moonlight.

He followed the man toward the end of the hall, and Richard unlocked a door, stepping out of sight for a moment. Marcus put his hand on the hilt of his sword before he heard the firesteel struck, the room brightening with a warm yellow glow a few moments later. He signaled for Simon to join him, then stepped inside.

"Where is this letter?" he asked Richard in a whisper, not wanting anyone to overhear their conversation, the walls no doubt thin.

Richard pointed at the floor and dropped to his knees, lifting up one of the boards, revealing a stash of what was most precious to him. He retrieved a piece of paper, then returned the board to its previous position. He handed the folded page to Marcus, who opened it and held it up to the lone light.

And nodded as it matched exactly what Simon had told him of the coachman's story.

"I will be keeping this."

53

Richard frowned, but acquiesced. "Of course."

"And I will need you to remain in Paris, at this address, in case I have further questions. I don't expect for more than a few days."

"Yes, sir."

Marcus stepped closer, pressing a finger against the man's chest. "Should you not remain, every Templar in Christendom will be looking for you."

Richard's eyes bulged and he started to shake. "You don't have to worry. I have nowhere to go."

De Montfort Residence
Paris, Kingdom of France

"What are you doing here?"

To say Marcus had been stunned to find Lord Charles at Sir Denys' residence would be an understatement. To find them both alive and unharmed, was an even bigger shock. Yet here both men were, clearly not on friendly terms, though calmer than he would have expected under the circumstances.

"Much has happened since we last spoke, Sir Marcus," replied Charles. "Sir Denys paid me a visit to explain his side of things, and after some discussion, I agreed to come here to see this portrait." He gestured toward the portrait of Denys and the imposter. "This is clearly not my wife, and is definitely the young woman you brought to my home earlier. I am confident now that Sir Denys did *not* have an affair with my wife, despite the charges that have now been laid." Charles glanced behind Marcus and Simon. "Where is the imposter? She must be brought to justice."

"She's dead."

Denys gasped, grabbing at his chest before collapsing into a nearby chair. "What? How?"

"Miss Girard was shot by an arrow the moment she stepped from her carriage. I gave chase, but the murderer had planned his escape well."

Denys grabbed at his hair, clearly overcome with grief. "I can't believe it!" He stared up at the others, his eyes red with tears. "I loved her!"

Charles was unsympathetic. "You mean you loved my wife!"

Denys shook his head. "No, I loved *her*. Who she pretended to be, I don't care. I cannot believe she didn't share my feelings. I confess, at first, I merely toyed with this woman I thought to be your wife, as I thought I might be able to use her advances to further my situation, but in time, real feelings developed. I love her, I mean, I loved her. I don't care who she actually was."

Charles sneered. "I should run you through for what you *thought* you were doing, but the Court will dismiss you as an idiot for having been deceived." He handed a piece of paper to Marcus. "But something more is going on. Several wives of the Court have been arrested for adultery tonight, and they are looking for mine. I think we have both been set up as part of whatever this is. My wife is innocent, but someone clearly wanted me and the Court to think otherwise. I have little doubt that when I return home, I will find members of the King's Personal Guard there to arrest her."

Marcus finished reading the message listing the charges, then handed it back to Charles. "Fortunately, no one knows where she is beyond those you sent to my farm."

Charles glanced away, a frown creasing his face. "I'm afraid that isn't actually true."

Marcus tensed. "What do you mean?"

"After our initial meeting, I immediately sent one of my servants to find out who you were. The Templar headquarters confirmed your identity, and your current location as Crécy-la-Chapelle, where my men had pursued my wife based upon her chambermaid's confession." He drew a deep breath. "My servant would know this, and perhaps has repeated it to others. As well, any number may have overheard him telling me what he found."

Marcus suppressed a curse. "So, if your staff are challenged as to her location, any number may reveal it."

Charles bowed his head. "Exactly."

Marcus pointed toward the door. "You must get home at once and prevent this, otherwise your wife's life may be forfeit, and if there is one innocent in this entire affair, it is her."

Charles turned to leave when Marcus interrupted him.

"And Lord Charles?"

"Yes?"

"I think you'll agree that your wife's chambermaid did nothing but save an innocent woman from becoming a victim of a jealous husband's revenge?"

Charles bristled, then nodded. "You are right, of course. I shall have her released at once."

Charles departed, and Marcus turned to Denys. "You said your artist drew sketches of Miss Girard in secret, in order to create the portrait."

Denys looked up at him, wiping his tears. "Yes."

"Do you have any of these?"

"Of course, I have them all. Why?"

"We have need of them."

Templar Barracks
Paris, Kingdom of France

"Did you notice anything unusual about those who've been arrested?"

Marcus stared at Sir Raimond de Comps as he relaxed by the fire, pleasantly surprised to have found his old friend staying at the barracks, and still awake at this ungodly hour. "I must confess I couldn't name one of them now, under threat of death. They meant nothing to me then, and even less now. Why?"

"This to me sounds like a political affair, not romantic. Think of what has happened. Four women, including your cousin, who we now know is innocent, stand accused of adultery, a heinous crime that not only demands a serious punishment for the parties involved, but also brings shame to the innocent husband, and with shame comes a weakening of status."

Marcus nodded. "Yes, this is true, but how can we know whether or not that is indeed what is happening here? These women are accused. I'm sure there is proof, and it will come out tomorrow."

Raimond smiled. "You are truly unfamiliar with how the process works, aren't you?"

Marcus chuckled. "I am out of my depth in these matters, yes. Please, my old friend, enlighten me."

Raimond leaned forward. "I can assure you, that only in the most dire of circumstances, would arrest warrants be issued at such an hour. And *never* for something as trivial as the dalliances of a few women."

"What are you saying?"

"I'm saying that this is political. Someone is making a move, and forcing the situation along at as quick a pace as they can, so that the damage will be done, and it will be irreparable, even if there are innocents like your cousin." He leaned even closer. "If I were a betting man—"

"Which of course you are not."

"—I'd be asking myself who has what to gain with these arrests, and in your case, in framing your cousin."

"Perhaps they're all innocent."

"Perhaps, though I'd be surprised someone would go to the risk of swearing out warrants for four women, without solid evidence of their crimes."

"Yet my cousin is absolutely innocent."

"Exactly. Someone wanted her caught up in this scandal, obviously to compromise her husband."

Marcus squeezed the bridge of his nose, his eyes drooping, it having been a long day. "I must clear my cousin's good name. The others aren't my concern."

Raimond wagged a finger at him, leaning back. "Your concern should be the truth. Pursue it to its end. If other innocents are caught up in this, then it is your duty as a Templar to uncover the truth, and ensure justice prevails."

Marcus yawned. "And here I thought the life of a farmer in France would be a quiet one."

Raimond smiled. "Clearly you were mistaken."

The door opened and Marcus glanced over to see a messenger standing there. "I'm looking for Sir Marcus de Rancourt."

Marcus waved his hand. "I am he."

The young man bowed. "An urgent message for you from Lord Charles de Rohan." He handed the folded paper over and Marcus opened it, his eyes widening at the revelation that indeed the King's Personal Guard had come to the residence, and the staff had told them about Crécy-la-Chapelle.

"Tell your master that I have received the message, and will take action to protect his wife."

"Yes, sir."

The messenger departed and Marcus rose.

"What is it?" asked Raimond, also standing.

"Trouble."

De Rancourt Residence
Crécy-la-Chapelle, Kingdom of France

Jeremy bolted upright on his bedroll, the blanket that barely kept him warm falling to the side as he listened for what woke him. Tanya was the first indicator, the dog barking incessantly, straining against her leash, the mastiff relegated to the half-finished barracks by Isabelle before she left for the evening.

A groggy David rolled over. "What is it?"

"I don't know."

A woman screamed and Jeremy kicked off his blanket and leaped to his feet, grabbing his sword and strapping the belt around his waist. He patted Tanya on the head. "Quiet, girl!"

The dog complied, though continued to growl as he retrieved his bow and shrugged a quiver of arrows over his shoulder, David doing the same. Jeremy rushed toward the home, two men on horseback visible, two more horses tied up at the post. He broke to the right so he could outflank them as David continued to the house. His friend approached using the home as a blind, then peered through the window of the bedroom normally occupied by Marcus.

The woman screamed again. "Help!"

That's it!

He drew an arrow and stretched his bow, rapidly loosing it without hesitation, the satisfying thud telling him he had hit his target, his second arrow already in the air before the first man fell from his saddle, an arrow embedded in his thigh. The other cried out, slumping forward as an arrow pierced his shoulder. Jeremy repositioned to get a good angle on the door, shouts from inside indicating the second man's cry had been heard by the others.

He had no idea who these men were, thus the two non-life threatening wounds he had inflicted. Though if those inside endangered the life of Lady Joanne, he might be left with no choice but to kill, even if they were only doing their job.

He glanced to his left to see David signaling in the moonlight that two more were coming. Jeremy sprinted closer, an arrow aimed at the two men now lying on the ground in agony, in case they mounted a defense. As he closed the gap to get a better shot at whoever might appear through the doorway, he could hear the struggles of Joanne inside continuing, and it enraged him.

One of the two he had already felled struggled to his feet and made for the doorway, and Jeremy put an end to that thought as he placed an arrow at the man's feet, causing him to jump back and lose his balance, collapsing into his horse who whinnied in protest.

"He's to your right!" shouted the man, and Jeremy cursed, wishing he had taken the man out properly, rather than given him the benefit of the doubt he might be guilty of only doing his duty.

Tanya bolted past David, toward the two men, her leash trailing behind her. Her first victim cried out in terror as snarls and growls filled the night air. Jeremy took the opportunity to close the gap further as a man appeared in the doorway. Tanya turned, barking, then leaped through the air, disappearing inside with the man for a moment, before reappearing, his arm in her jaws as she dragged him into view.

Jeremy put an arrow in the man's thigh as a fourth man rushed outside and grabbed the reins of his horse. David pressed a sword against the man's as Jeremy rushed to join him.

"Who sent you?" demanded David.

The man slowly turned, his hands held high. "The King!"

"Then have him take up his business with our master!"

The man spat. "You'll all be dead before the day is out for interfering with the King's business!"

Tanya growled, David holding her by the collar. "Be off with you, before I let her loose on you!"

The lone unscathed man helped the others back on their horses, then the four left without saying another word. David monitored their retreat as Jeremy rushed inside, the sobs of Lady Joanne continuing. He found her in the corner of the kitchen, her top torn exposing a breast, her cheeks stained with tears. He quickly found a blanket and brought it to her as David entered.

"They're gone."

Jeremy covered the woman up, then he stepped back, unsure of what to do.

David spoke first, in a whisper. "This was no ordinary arrest. They intended to defile her."

Jeremy stole another glance at the woman, nodding. "What should we do?"

"We can't stay here. They'll be back, and in greater numbers."

64

THE PARISIAN ADULTERESS

"But where will we go?"

"I don't know, but we have to leave now."

Rue Saint-Honoré
Paris, Kingdom of France

"I'm concerned about David and Jeremy, and my cousin, of course."

Simon nodded, riding slowly alongside Marcus as they weaved their way through the streets of Paris, the common man and woman of the neighborhood they found themselves in, now awake and filling it with the sounds and deeds of life.

Much different from the aristocratic estates they had frequented yesterday. It reminded Marcus more of the Holy Land, and though his opinion of the city wasn't favorable, perhaps he might spend some time here, to feel more at home.

Though the farm occupied almost every moment of every day.

"It is unsettling that there has been no word. Surely the messenger has reached them by now."

Marcus grunted. "It was late, and dark. They would have to take their time, though I agree, they should have been there some time ago. Hopefully, we'll have received word when we are finished with our business here."

Simon rode ahead slightly, breaking apart a gaggle of beggars threatening to impede their progress. "I'm sure they're all right. They're not exactly recruits."

"No, but we have no idea how many were sent to arrest my cousin. If the odds are even, they can hold their own, but they are not knights."

Simon frowned. "True." He turned in his saddle toward Marcus. "What do you want to do? Return to the farm?"

Marcus thought for a moment then shook his head. "No. By the time we reach there, anything that was going to happen would have already. If they prevailed, they will seek safety somewhere, likely at a Templar commandry. If they failed, they are either dead or arrested. If they are dead, then there is nothing we can do about it now. If they have been arrested, then they will be brought here as part of this trial, and we will deal with it then." He sighed. "No, the best course of action is to forge ahead and determine what exactly is going on here. Even if my cousin is dead, as Sir Raimond pointed out last night, it is our duty to protect *all* the innocents, and I have a feeling these other three women are guilty of nothing but being married to the wrong men."

"There's the market," said Simon, pointing ahead. "I think we're here."

Marcus dismounted, retrieving the sketches provided by Sir Denys last night, handing one to Simon. It didn't take long before a shopkeeper recognized her.

"Yes, she comes here all the time. Melanie, her name is. Why? Has she stolen from ya?"

Marcus shook his head. "No, nothing like that. Do you know where she lives?"

The man pointed across the street, several buildings down. "Talk to the lady of the house there. I think your young woman was renting a room."

Marcus bowed slightly. "Thank you for your help."

"No problem, sir, no problem."

Marcus and Simon led their horses to the building in question, the ground floor occupied by a fishmonger, leaving Marcus to wonder how anyone could stand to live above the smell.

"Gentlemen, can I interest you in some fresh fish?"

Marcus had to question the word "fresh." "Not today, I'm afraid. We'd like to talk to someone about a young woman who lives here. Miss Girard?" He showed the sketch.

"Oh yes, she lives upstairs, third floor." He jabbed a knife over his shoulder. "Go in back and ask my wife. She handles the boarders." He turned, shouting. "Wife! Visitors!"

"Send them back!"

Marcus smiled. "Thanks." He stepped into the back, taking a moment for his eyes to adjust to the dim interior as a shadow approached. He resisted the urge to draw his sword, reminding himself that Paris was not the Holy Land, and that not all figures in the shadows were intent on doing harm.

A portly woman emerged, a smile on her face as she wiped her hands dry on a threadbare apron. "Ooh, a Templar Knight! To what do we owe the honor?"

Marcus bowed deeply, giving the woman a thrill, he was certain, and a story to tell her friends for years to come. "Ma'am, we're sorry to disturb you, but we are seeking information on a woman whom we believe lived upstairs. Melanie Girard."

The woman's eyes widened. "Melanie? What business could Templar Knights possibly have with a woman like that?" She elbowed him. "Looking to break some vows, are we?"

It took a moment for Marcus to understand why Simon was snickering, and his cheeks flushed once he did. "No, ma'am, nothing untoward, I assure you. Unfortunately, I have some bad news. Miss Girard is dead, murdered last night, and we are trying to determine why."

The woman gasped, taking a step back as a hand flew to her mouth. "Husband! Melanie is dead!"

"What?" The fishmonger rushed inside, his eyes wide. "What did you say? Did you say Melanie is dead?"

Marcus frowned. "I'm afraid so. We were hoping to see her room."

The woman drew a deep breath. "I-I'll show you."

"Are you all right, love?" asked the husband, placing a hand on her shoulder. She patted it and nodded, then pointed toward a set of stairs to the right.

"Follow me." She led them up two flights of stairs, the husband returning to hawking his wares, then opened a door decorated with a hand painted lily. The woman stepped inside and threw open the curtains, sunlight pouring in, revealing a room filled with things far finer than anyone living in such a place should possess.

It was definitely Melanie Girard's room, and she was clearly paid well for her services.

"Sir."

Marcus glanced over his shoulder to see Simon pointing at a piece of paper sitting on a dresser. He stepped over and picked it up, reading what appeared to be the instructions for her latest meeting with Sir Denys. He frowned as he removed the letter given to

69

them by the coachman from his pocket, comparing the handwriting. "They appear to be written by the same hand, though I'm no expert."

"And does this new letter tell us anything?"

"Only that her instructions were quite explicit. She was to, umm, sleep with him again, declare her undying love, and question him as to what should be done with her husband."

Simon frowned. "What a lovely character this one must be."

Marcus agreed. "He is eloquent and educated, by the looks of this. There's no way a man of means is coming into this neighborhood unnoticed." He turned to the landlady. "Ma'am, how are these letters being delivered?"

"Once a week a man arrived with a letter for Melanie."

"Can you describe him?"

"He's always dressed shabbily. No one would give him a second glance. But I always thought there was something odd about him."

Marcus' eyebrows climbed. "Yes?"

"He always smelled far too good for someone from these parts."

"Did he ever say anything?"

"Never a word, not even her name. He would simply hand me or my husband the letter with her name on the front, then leave. If it weren't for his lack of smell, I would have thought he was paid to deliver them."

"Anything unique about him?"

She shrugged. "Nothing I can think of."

"What did he look like?"

Another shrug. "Dunno. He always wore a hood that covered his face, and he'd be here mere moments."

"Did Miss Girard ever leave him anything?"

The woman shook her head.

"And how did Miss Girard seem when she received the letters?"

"Happy, I should think, as they clearly contained coins." She tapped her chin. "Though, come to think of it, the last few times she did seem out of sorts."

"How long has this been going on?"

"A couple of months, I should think."

Marcus glanced about the room, searching for anything that might prompt another question. He paused. "Did she seem surprised at the first message?"

The landlady shook her head. "No, I got the distinct impression she was anticipating it."

Marcus nodded, turning to Simon. "That means whoever she was dealing with, met her somewhere else." He turned back to the landlady. "Any idea where that might be?"

The woman grunted. "All the girls of her type end up at the Three Moons at one point or another."

Marcus regarded her. "Her type?"

The woman stared at him, her expression as if he had said something incredibly naïve. "She's a prostitute! Didn't you know that?" She waved her hand around the room as Marcus controlled his jaw. "And a fairly high-priced one, considering the fine clothes I've seen her in of late." She raised a finger.

71

"You know, since she's been receiving these letters, she hasn't been making merry with her lot."

Simon grunted. "Not surprising, considering her newfound wealth. She could become a target."

Marcus agreed. "Where might we find this Three Moons?"

The woman stepped to the window and pointed down the street. "Just out the door and to your left. Follow the filth a few hundred paces. You can't miss it."

The Three Moons Tavern
Paris, Kingdom of France

The smell was the first thing to strike Marcus, then the sheer acreage of exposed flesh. Women with skirts hiked above their knees, bosoms pouring out of their tops, and no shame or modesty on display anywhere.

And the men loved it.

It was unlike any establishment he had ever before experienced.

He had heard of places like these, of course, though they were relegated to the darkest corners in the Holy Land, as there were more pious men than not in those parts. But here, in Paris, it was in plain sight on a busy street, and nobody paid it any mind.

God has been abandoned by these people.

Though he knew *He* would never abandon *them*.

All in good time.

"So, what do you think?"

Simon's eyes were wide, his vows not as absolute as Marcus', though strictly adhered to as far as he knew. "Umm, I'm finding I can't think straight after the stench of fish earlier."

"I'd prefer fish to this."

"Then you have truly been touched, sir. *Nothing* is worse than the smell of fish." He grinned as he looked around. "But I'm beginning to forget about it."

Marcus chuckled. "I'm glad I brought you. David and Jeremy would be of absolutely no use to me."

73

Simon laughed. "The poor boys would have fainted by now, or left the Order altogether." He pointed at a group of women cloistered in the corner. "How about we start with them?"

Marcus nodded and they strode deeper into the establishment, a hush falling over the proceedings as their Templar markings were finally noticed. He glared at one man about to open his mouth, and the man paled, silenced before the first syllable could be sounded.

Marcus produced one of the sketches of Melanie Girard. "Excuse me, ladies."

"Ooh, ladies! Who's the gentleman, now?"

Marcus smiled. "We're looking for this woman." He showed the sketch. "Her name is Melanie Girard. Do any of you know her?"

"I'm sorry, Sir Knight, but I think she's out of your price range now, what with you taking a vow of poverty. Or have you forgotten that one too!"

The table roared with laughter, immediately joined by the bar. Simon bristled beside him, but Marcus chose a different tack, tossing his head back and joining in. "I'm sure any of you fine ladies are out of my price range, should I be looking, but I'm not." He wiped the smile from his face. "I'm afraid I am the bearer of bad news, but only to those who knew her."

This elicited the response he wanted. "We know her. Or at least did. She hasn't been about in months." The woman eyeballed him. "What is this bad news you speak of?"

"She's been murdered."

Gasps from the table and those within earshot confirmed to him that they knew the girl. "How?"

"That doesn't matter right now, what does, is who her current employer was. Have you seen her with anyone different? Anyone unusual?"

Heads shook then a redhead near the wall pounded her drink onto the table. "What about that bloke she met here that time?"

Sounds of recollection and a hurried, whispered discussion followed before Marcus was made privy to the details. "A few months back, she came in, and rather than join us, told us she was meeting someone, someone important. She sat at her own table, and he arrived a short while later. They spoke for about a quarter hour, then left together. We haven't really seen much of her since."

"Can you tell us anything about him?"

The woman shrugged. "Not particularly. He wore a robe that covered him from head to toe. I couldn't see his face. He was definitely not from these parts, though."

"What makes you say that?"

"Dressed too finely, and when they left, they climbed into a carriage." She motioned at the customers with disdain. "None of this lot have carriages."

"Anything unique about it? Any markings?"

"There was probably a crest on the door, but I honestly can't remember."

Marcus frowned. "That would have made it too easy, I suppose. Anything else you ladies can remember?"

Another leaned forward. "Didn't he have a cane?"

"Yes, that's right!" cried the redhead. "He had a limp. Quite bad, if I remember correctly."

"Did he seem elderly? Frail?"

The women all shook their heads, the redhead replying for them. "Not at all. He seemed healthy enough. In fact, he moved quite quickly, despite the limp."

Marcus bowed. "Thank you for your help, ladies."

A round of over the top responses devolved into laughter as Marcus and Simon left, Marcus drawing several deep cleansing breaths when they were far enough away, ridding himself of the filth they had just experienced.

"That man you chased, do you think he needed a cane?"

Marcus shrugged. "He certainly handled his horse well. I would have to say no, though if practiced enough, anything is possible. God knows I've seen men who could barely walk, handle a horse in battle as if they were one."

"So, we could be looking for a man with a limp, or not." Simon sighed. "I don't know if we're any further ahead than we were yesterday."

"Unfortunately, I have to agree."

"Then what now?"

"There's a question I need answered, that I didn't think to ask our coachman."

"And what's that?"

"Who delivered the letter and payment?"

Coachman Richard's Residence
Paris, Kingdom of France

Marcus knocked yet again, and still there was no answer. The man could be out, but the landlady downstairs had said he hadn't come down yet. It was possible she had missed him, though he had his doubts. Melanie Girard had been murdered, and as far as they knew, the coachman was the only person left who was involved in this conspiracy.

Someone could be tying up loose ends.

He tried the door and found it unlocked. Pushing it open, he sighed with disappointment at the sight before him. The coachman was dead, bled out from the stomach, likely by a blade shoved deep and twisted, his body lying on the floor in front of the door. Whoever had killed him had probably stabbed him immediately upon entering, the door perhaps opened by the victim himself.

"This is a bloody mess," muttered Simon.

"Yes." Marcus kneeled by the body and felt the man's cheek. "He's still warm. This didn't happen too long ago."

He stepped out of the room, closing the door, then hurried down the stairs, followed by Simon. He flagged down the landlady, about to enter one of the rooms. "Ma'am, a word."

"Yes? Did you find your friend?"

"We did, ma'am. Did he have any visitors this morning?"

77

"Yes, yes he did. A very generous man, in fact."

Marcus regarded her. "Why do you say that?"

"When I asked his business, he tossed me several coins, and asked what room your friend was in. I told him, he went to see your friend, then returned a short while later and left."

"Did he say anything when he left?"

"Nothing."

"Was he carrying a cane?" asked Simon.

The woman shook her head. "No, I think I should remember that. Why?"

"We've heard mention of a limp."

"Well, this man didn't have one." The woman's mouth slowly opened. "But now that you mention it, I did hear him express some discomfort when he took that first step. It's a little higher than usual."

Marcus eyed it, remembering from the night before that it was indeed almost twice the height it should be. If someone were not yet fully recovered from some injury, it could prove a challenge. "How long has he lived here?"

"Years. An excellent tenant. I never had a problem with him. I always felt he could do better, but he seemed content to live here. He kept to himself for the most part, and rarely entertained."

"Did he ever have any visitors? Family? Friends?"

Simon leaned in. "A lady?"

The woman's head shook until Simon's interjection. "Actually, a lady did come here once, a few months ago, though how much of a lady she could be, I don't know. A woman visiting a man in his room? I can think of only one purpose for that!"

78

Marcus suppressed a smile. "Could you describe her?"

"Overdressed."

"Excuse me?"

"You know, trying to be a lady, but not quite managing it. Her bearing wasn't right. She was dressed well, but I doubt she was born into the money she wore."

Simon leaned closer to Marcus. "That sounds like our girl."

And it did, which suggested their coachman had been lying about his relationship with his passenger. "Anything else you can tell us?"

"Brunette. Maybe forty."

Simon grunted. "Definitely not our girl."

Marcus agreed. "How long did she visit him?"

"Perhaps a quarter hour if that."

"Not very long for anything untoward."

Simon cleared his throat. "Some men are faster than others, sir."

Marcus gave his sergeant a look. "I'll yield to your expertise on the matter." He returned his attention to the landlady. "And you've never seen this woman since?"

"Not here."

Marcus eyed him. "What do you mean?"

"Oh, I've seen her about."

"Where?"

She shrugged. "Nowhere specific. Just in the street."

"When was the last time you saw her?"

79

"Perhaps a week ago, maybe two." She smiled. "I remember now! The last time I saw her was at the Swan. It's a tavern a short distance from here. Ask there, they may know who she is." She leaned closer, lowering her voice. "But watch yourselves. It's a bad lot that hangs out there."

The Swan Tavern
Paris, Kingdom of France

"You two lost?"

Marcus ignored the jabs at their expense as they entered yet another establishment of questionable repute, this time with the intention of simply asking the proprietor for his assistance, rather than the riffraff occasioning his business.

"We don't serve sacramental wine here!"

Even Simon chuckled at that one as they reached the bar.

"What can I do for a Templar Knight?" asked the man, his eyes bloodshot, his features gaunt from enjoying his own offerings a little too much.

"We're looking for a woman."

"Aren't we all!" he roared, the bar joining in. "I thought Templars were sworn to keep their swords sheathed?"

Simon snorted, Marcus ignoring the insult. "She's possibly in her forties. Brunette. Dresses above her station."

The barkeeper lowered his voice. "Oh, you're speaking of Simone." He leaned in closer. "What business could you possibly have with her?"

"None that concerns you!" muttered Simon.

Marcus held out a hand, calming the man. "Why? What is her business?"

"All things nefarious, I assure you. If there's anything you want in these parts, she's the one to see."

81

"An odd business for a woman."

The man shook his head. "Oh, she didn't start the business, her husband did. But when smallpox took him, she stepped in to take over." He frowned. "A little too eagerly, if you ask me."

"What makes you say that?"

The barkeeper lowered his voice further, leaning in closer. "She's a vicious one. If you're going to do business with her, then I'd watch my back."

Marcus nodded. "Thanks for the warning. Any idea where we can find her?"

The man lowered his voice further still. "I'll give you the address, but you never heard it from me, understood?"

Marcus could see the fear in the man's eyes, and wondered how justified it was, though it was clear he wouldn't be given the information he needed were he to dismiss it. "Understood."

Simone Thibault Residence
Paris, Kingdom of France

"We're here to see Mrs. Thibault."

A brick wall of a man filled the doorway, the scowl so deep, a smile might physically hurt him. "What possible business could a Templar Knight and his sergeant have with her?"

Marcus smiled pleasantly. "Don't you think she should be permitted to hear our business herself?"

The man grunted, unswayed. "She's a busy woman."

"I have no doubt. But does she know she is in extreme danger?"

The man eyed the two of them. "Not from the likes of you two, I'm sure."

"Of course not. But two people are already dead, and at least one of them had business dealings with your mistress. I think she would want to know that."

"Why don't you just give me the message, and I'll pass it on?"

Marcus shook his head. "I have questions that only she can answer. Now, are you going to let me see her, or do I have to tell her she needs a new doorman?"

The man's eyes narrowed. "And why would she need a new one?"

"Because you'll be dead." Marcus drew his sword a few inches.

A woman screamed from within, and the doorman's eyes bulged. Marcus shoved past him, followed by Simon, the lumbering behemoth close behind.

"Where?" demanded Marcus, tossing the question over his shoulder, another terrified cry coming from upstairs the answer. He rushed up the stairs in front of him then stormed down a long, narrow hallway, a commotion coming from the end of it. He kicked open the closed door, his sword drawn, as he took in the scene.

A woman was on the floor, her arms raised in self-defense, as a man was already half out the window. Marcus charged toward him but he jumped clear, running along the rooftop, the roofing tiles sliding out from under his feet before he leaped to the ground and out of sight. Marcus made to go after him when he heard a horse whinny, then the sound of it breaking out into a gallop, pedestrians on the street shouting in protest as the man successfully made his escape.

Marcus stifled a curse then turned to Simon. "If we were looking for a man who needed a cane, he wasn't it, or no longer needs it."

"Why would you say that?"

Marcus turned to the woman, her doorman helping her into a nearby chair. She appeared flustered, and she winced as she examined a cut on the top of her left hand.

"You were lucky to have survived, Mrs. Thibault, unless his intent was not to kill you."

Thibault frowned. "Oh, he intended, all right. He definitely intended." She pulled up her sleeves, revealing metal armor wrapping her lower arms. "He didn't anticipate that I was prepared for such an eventuality."

Marcus chuckled in appreciation. "A wise precaution in your line of work."

Thibault regarded him. "And what do you know of my line of work?"

Marcus bowed slightly. "Little, except that you were acquainted with a man who is now dead." He paused. "But why did you ask about what I said? About the cane?"

She gestured toward the window, then dabbed at the cut with a handkerchief. "This man that just attacked me. I've had dealings with him over the past several months. When I first met him, he employed a cane, but today he had none."

"And you're sure it was the same man?"

She eyed him. "I'm not a fool, though I must confess I've never seen more than his chin. I recognized his voice, of course, so I know it's the same man."

Marcus paused with a thought. "If you heard it again, out of context, would you recognize it?"

Thibault shrugged. "Perhaps, though context is sometimes everything, and he was attempting to disguise it." She wrapped the handkerchief around her hand then switched to a seat behind a large, ornate desk. "Now, what is your business with me?"

"You had dealings with a coachman named Richard."

Her eyes widened slightly. "What of it?"

"May I ask what your business with him was?"

The woman sighed. "If you had asked me an hour ago, I would have said no, but as my business with Richard was related to the man who just tried to kill me, I will tell you." She paused as a maid entered the room with a bowl of water and several clean towels, immediately setting to work cleaning the wounded hand, Thibault ignoring her as if the cut were no matter. "Our mystery man hired me to find him a trustworthy coachman, and a beautiful woman of rather exacting specifications."

"Exacting?"

"Yes. Height, weight, age, skin tone, hair color. All had to be quite exact. Furthermore, she had to be trained to act like a lady."

Marcus already knew the answer, but he asked the question regardless. "And you found such a woman?"

"Yes, in all regards but age."

"And was her name Melanie Girard?"

Thibault's eyes widened again. "Yes! How did you know?"

"Ma'am, both of these people you hired, have been murdered."

The woman uttered a string of curses that would have made any sailor proud, enough to cause even Simon to shift uncomfortably. She stabbed a finger at the open window. "I knew I shouldn't have gotten involved with him. Whenever you deal with the aristocracy, you know it will never end well. I mean, what was I—"

Marcus held up a hand. "Sorry, aristocracy? How do you know this man is aristocracy?"

She huffed. "I can tell. They have a distinct way about them, and that way they talk? You can pick one out in a mob if you listen carefully enough. It's unmistakable. Only aristocracy spoke the way this one did."

Marcus' exposure to aristocracy was limited, most of it over the past two days, and several weeks ago in the King's Court. And he had to admit, they spoke far finer French than most he had encountered.

And then there was the arrogance.

Most he had encountered spoke with a tone that he wasn't even certain they were aware of. It was condescending, as if they knew they were better than anyone else that didn't share their station, though he suspected that was true of any aristocracy in the world.

He stepped back as the maid finished treating the wound, taking the now pink water away. "How were you able to train Melanie to act as a lady? I had the opportunity to speak to her, and the transformation was quite remarkable."

"It wasn't too difficult. She simply had to be reminded of what she already knew. She had grown up working in the household of a baron, until he died without a male heir, leaving the estate to be torn apart by distant relations. When the new master took a liking to her with the back of his hand, she fled to the streets. That's where I found her, and put her to work."

"As a prostitute."

Thibault shrugged. "It's a living."

"Not much of one."

A burst of air escaped her lips. "I dare say she had a better life these past several months than she ever had or would."

"Except that now she's dead."

Thibault frowned. "True, but everyone has to die at some point. Better to do it with some pleasant memories, rather than nothing but misery."

Marcus had to admit it was a difficult argument to counter, and thought of the room he had found, filled with beautiful things that little girls loved, something he was learning through helping raise Angeline.

You must give that little girl good memories.

"You said she was murdered. When?"

Marcus focused on the woman again, his train of thought momentarily lost. "Last night, when we figured out what she was up to."

"And what *was* she up to?"

Marcus' eyebrows shot up. "You don't know?"

Thibault shook her head. "I have no idea. I was hired to find her and train her, nothing more. Once she was ready, I notified him."

Marcus' heart beat a little faster. "You notified him? How?"

She motioned at the doorman. "Enzo left a note under a specific pew at St. Severin Church."

"And how long was it before you heard from him."

"The very next day."

Simon grunted. "That suggests he, or someone under his employ, checked regularly."

Marcus agreed. "At what time did your man leave the note?"

She shrugged, motioning toward the pile of muscle and sinew. "Ask him yourself."

It spoke. "I don't remember specifically, but it was in the evening, after dark."

"What day of the week?"

He shrugged. "Dunno. Don't remember."

Marcus turned to Thibault. "Do you?"

88

"No idea, though it wasn't a Sunday, that's all I know."

"Why?"

"Our girl was a good Catholic. We never trained on Sundays."

Marcus turned to Enzo. "Specifically, which pew."

"Facing the altar, far left, third one from the front. There's a gap between the wood."

Marcus nodded. "I think that's our next stop."

Simon agreed. "I could use some time in a church, after what we've seen today."

Thibault leaned forward. "And what is this business that I have myself mixed up in?"

"The woman you found was hired to impersonate a lady, and then to have an affair with a member of the King's Court, pretending to be the wife of a rival."

Thibault's eyes shot wide. "Who?"

"Their names are unimportant. Let us just say that the scandal is already significant, as others have been implicated. I dare say it will shake the very foundations of the Court."

Thibault paled, the first true hint of fear he had observed in her. "If someone went to such trouble, then they must indeed be powerful."

"Yes, and they have already killed two of those involved, and made an attempt on your life."

She absentmindedly ran a finger over her bandaged hand. "Then you think I am still in danger?"

"Absolutely. If I were you, I'd immediately make myself scarce until such time as my safety could be assured."

She stared at him. "By whom? You?"

Marcus bowed slightly. "I intend to uncover the truth, and in so doing, hopefully bring to justice the man who now threatens your life."

"And in the meantime?"

"Do you have someplace to go?"

She laughed. "If anyone here gets wind that the aristocracy wants me dead, they're liable to try and kill me themselves in the hopes of collecting some reward."

Marcus frowned. "You have no friends or family?"

This time even her man laughed. "One does not make friends in my business, and my only family is dead."

Marcus sighed, thinking for a moment. This woman was in danger, and despite her profession, deserved protection, not to mention the fact she may yet possess information that might help him. She was the only person still alive that had even met the man behind this, and he still hoped she might recognize his voice when the time came.

He smiled at an idea. "I might actually have the perfect place for you to hide, if you are willing to humble yourself until these matters are settled."

She eyed him. "Where?"

"With a friend." He motioned toward her. "If you want my help, then we must leave immediately. Take only what you need, and a heavy purse."

She rose, eying him suspiciously. "Why?"

"Because your host is extremely poor, and as payment for him providing you with shelter, you will pay generously for your accommodations."

She grunted. "Sounds like a scheme if I ever heard one."

"Ma'am, not all are like you."

She laughed. "And a good thing! If they were, I'd have no one to profit from."

Durant Residence
Paris, Kingdom of France

Thomas Durant's stomach growled again, the starving protests of his body now going unnoticed, his mind numb to the warning signals sent it. He stretched out his arm, remarkably emaciated compared to just a few days ago, yet still with enough meat to keep him going.

Something had to give.

He couldn't stay like this much longer.

He'd soon be dead.

Good.

It was what he wanted. At least that's what he kept telling himself. With his father dead, what did he have to live for? This was a wretched existence, and he was tired of it. At least with his father around, they had an income, and no matter how meager it was, it had provided enough for them to keep their bellies full and their bones warm enough.

But now there was no money, no food, and he had resorted to burning the furniture, as the days grew colder and the nights longer. The charity displayed by his neighbors had waned then dried up. Some of it was fatigue on their part, but most of it was his fault. He had taken to consuming all the alcohol, and cursing those that arrived with food rather than drink.

And now he had nothing.

No mother, no father, no living relations that he was aware of, no prospects, and no skills beyond reading and writing, nearly useless in these parts.

And soon, he had no doubt, no roof over his head.

The glint of a knife lying on the floor caught his eye, last used to cut a loaf of bread left by the neighbor across the street, a good friend to his father. It was sharp. All the knives in the house were, his father a stickler for a sharp blade. It could do the job. It could end things quickly. One plunge into the stomach, or a slice across the wrist, and it would all be over.

Just one quick slice of the wrist.

The stomach would be too painful, but the wrist, that could easily be done. It would hurt for but a moment, then he could simply relax and let his body take care of the rest.

And when it was over, he'd see his father and mother once again.

Only if they're condemned to Hell.

He closed his eyes, and they burned with shame. To take one's life was the ultimate sin, and he had an option, an option his pride prevented him from taking.

But why?

The offer had been genuine, he was sure of it. It would be a hard life, though a good life, and perhaps could lead to something even better should he choose.

But he had to choose.

He had to stop wallowing in self-pity, and reach out and grab that offer of security, a security his father had provided until a few weeks ago.

He had to leave this wretched place, and make for the farm where food, warmth, and companionship awaited him, for if he didn't, the elements, or his weakness of spirit, would end him once and for all.

He sighed, closing his eyes, his mind displaying an image of the proud Templar Knight who had been nothing but kind to him, despite barely knowing him.

The offer was genuine.

But toiling on a farm? He couldn't even imagine what that would be like. And to leave his home, the only one he had ever known? It would be like abandoning his mother and father, and every memory they had built over the years.

It felt like a betrayal.

They would want you to survive.

His shoulders shook as a wave of shame and desperation swept over him.

"Oh God, please help me! Please tell me what to do!"

His parched mouth barely gave voice to the words, yet they weren't meant for the ears of mortals, but for the Lord above, someone in whose faith he felt slipping away by the moment.

I don't know what to do!

Yet he did.

He had no choice.

He had to leave everything he had known his entire life, and start anew.

He had to survive.

He curled into a ball, covering himself with his father's threadbare blanket in front of the embers of a dying fire, his shoulders shaking from the cold, the hunger, and the shame.

When someone knocked on the door.

Durant Residence
Paris, Kingdom of France

Marcus stepped back from the door, glancing at Simon, who had been here before. "Was it like this last time?"

Simon shook his head, pointing at several boards covering the windows. "This was a place open for business. Now it almost appears as if abandoned."

Marcus flagged down a woman passing by. "Do you know if the boy still lives here? Thomas Durant?"

She nodded. "Aye, if he still lives, he's inside. I haven't seen him in days though. Poor thing. He's taking the death of his father very hard."

Marcus bowed slightly. "Thank you." He rapped on the door several more times. "Master Durant. This is Sir Marcus de Rancourt. I have a favor to ask of you."

He placed his ear to the door, listening for any sign of life on the other side, but it was impossible to tell with the din of daily life surrounding them. He shook his head and raised a boot to kick open the door, the safety of the boy now in question, when it opened a crack, a sliver of an emaciated face appearing.

He forced a smile, hiding his shock at the change only a few weeks had brought. "Master Durant, do you remember me?"

The young man nodded.

"May we come in?"

95

He still said nothing, but pulled the door open, stepping aside. Marcus entered the dingy interior, Simon and Thibault following, her doorman, Enzo, left behind despite protests.

"You expect me to stay here?"

Marcus gave Thibault a look, silencing her. "You don't look well, son. When was the last time you ate?"

He shrugged, his reply barely a whisper. "At least a few days. Maybe a week."

Marcus shook his head, frowning. He motioned to Simon. "Take off your markings so you blend in a little more. Get us food, drink, and wood for the fire."

Simon began disrobing. "And with what bounty shall I pay for all this?"

Marcus chuckled then beckoned Thibault. "It's time to contribute."

She shook her head, muttering about the environment as she fetched several coins. She handed them to Simon, who left immediately. Marcus sat Thomas down in one of the two remaining chairs, Thibault taking the other as she surveyed the surroundings with disdain.

"I have a favor to ask of you."

Thomas looked up at him. "What? As you can see, I'm not in a position to actually offer much."

Marcus smiled. "But you have the one thing I require."

"And that is?"

"Shelter." He motioned at Thibault. "This is Mrs. Thibault. She requires a place to stay where nobody knows her, while Simon and I try to find those who would harm her and others more innocent."

Thomas regarded the woman for a moment. "What's going on?"

"The less you know the better, but I will let you know everything eventually, I assure you. The good news for you, is that Mrs. Thibault is a woman of some means, and she intends to pay you handsomely"—she laughed—"for your sacrifice." Marcus looked about. "It should be enough to get you back on your feet for a short while, anyway."

Thomas shrugged, waving a hand at the surroundings. "As you can see, I'm in no position to say no."

"Excellent." Marcus turned to Thibault. "I think a down payment would be a kind gesture at this moment."

Her frown deepened, but several more coins were produced and placed on the table. Thomas' eyes bulged and his stomach growled.

Marcus leaned in toward the woman, lowering his voice. "You have a chance for redemption, madam. Be a good Christian and help him while you are here. If I hear he is mistreated in any way, I will deliver you to justice myself."

Thibault's annoyed expression eased as she nodded, staring at Thomas. "You're lucky he reminds me of my husband when he was a young man. So handsome." She looked at Marcus. "Don't worry, I'll get him back on his feet again. But make sure you let me know the moment you bring my would-be killer to justice. I don't want to spend a moment more than I must in such…a place."

Marcus smiled slightly. "I shall. And keep a low profile, madam. Turning this humble home into anything other than what it is, will simply draw undue attention to you."

She scowled. "I'm not a fool."

"Yet here you are."

She sighed, her shoulders sagging. "Yes, yet here I am. And what will you do now?"

"The less you know, the better." Marcus turned to Thomas. "Young man, when my business in Paris is done, I would like you to consider my previous offer. Your situation here seems grave, and you have an option that will at least get you through the winter, and give you time to decide what is best for you."

Thomas' slowly nodded. "I-I must confess, I've been thinking of that. There's…" His voice cracked, and tears filled his eyes. "There's nothing for me here now."

Marcus put a hand on the young man's shoulder and squeezed. "Then join us on the farm. There is plenty of food, a roof over your head, and the laughter of children at play and the camaraderie of men at work fills the air."

Thomas sighed, tears pouring down his cheeks. "That-that sounds wonderful."

Marcus smiled. "Then it is settled. When this is over, you will join us."

St. Severin Church
Paris, Kingdom of France

"Thomas didn't look well."

Marcus sighed as he tied up his horse alongside Simon's. "No, he didn't. I fear he may not be long for this earth should he not follow through with his acceptance of my offer."

"To join us on the farm?"

"Yes."

"I pray he does, otherwise I agree." Simon glanced up at the impressive structure that was St. Severin Church. "I think the good Lord was guiding us today. If we hadn't had need of Thomas' home, he might have died within days."

Marcus nodded. "Well, if need be, I'll strap him to the back of my horse. No matter what happens, I'm not leaving him like that. He's a fine young man who just needs a push in the right direction. Once he's back on his feet and thinking straight, he can decide what he wants to do. For now, someone has to tell him."

Simon smiled. "Our farm is getting a little crowded, don't you think?"

Marcus chuckled. "It is, but part of me feels like that is a good thing. We have more than enough land to feed everyone, and perhaps this new home we're building can replace the brotherhood we have lost."

Simon frowned slightly, his response barely a murmur. "Perhaps."

Marcus let it be, making a note to remember to talk to his sergeant about his feelings later. His men had eagerly agreed to stay with him out of a sense of loyalty, but he didn't want anyone remaining on the farm against their will. If any one of them wanted to return to the Order, and live out their lives as they had sworn to do, he would never hold it against them.

Though it would hurt him deeply.

Every day, part of him yearned to return to the Holy Land and serve out his days among his brothers, and he was certain the others felt the same. Yet he was the only one who couldn't leave. He *had* to remain behind. There was no way he would abandon his niece and nephew, and now Pierre. His future was written.

But the others' weren't.

A conversation is definitely in order.

They quickly made their way to the pew in question, finding no message tucked into the gap, though that didn't surprise him. He spotted a priest nearby, and beckoned him over. The old man joined them, bowing slightly.

"It is rare to see a Templar Knight here. Are you here just for prayer, or do you have a purpose?"

Marcus bowed. "Prayer is always a purpose, however today we have another." He gestured toward the end of the pew. "Have you noticed anything strange over the past few months? Anyone out of place, who paid particular attention to the end of this pew, as if searching for something?"

The priest chuckled, shaking his head. "I'm afraid, my son, that my memory and eyesight are beginning to fail me, though even if they weren't, I doubt my answer would be any different. This church fills every day, and this pew so close to the front is quite popular. Countless people sit here on countless occasions, I'm afraid."

Marcus frowned. "That was what I feared. And in the evenings?"

"You'll find our doors always open. Unfortunately, I've noticed nothing strange even among the Lord's strays."

"Very well. Thank you for your time, Father."

The man bowed then took his leave, as Marcus eyed the altar before them. "I think we should take a few moments to pray for guidance."

Simon nodded. "And should the good Lord leave it up to us?"

"Then I think we should present ourselves to the King's Court to hear these charges. My understanding is they are to be formally announced within the hour."

Palais de la Cité
Paris, Kingdom of France

The gathered members of the King's Court and their honored guests seemed in fine spirits as Marcus watched the tragedy unfold. The charges were read, the accused named, and those in attendance were giddy with delight at the salaciousness of the crimes.

It was theatre.

Entertainment.

But it was real lives on the line, including his cousin's, who was named, though not presented, the prosecutor indicating she was still at large, though perhaps already in custody, a unit dispatched last night to arrest her in Crécy-la-Chapelle.

It sent a shiver up and down his spine, as they still had not received word from David and Jeremy. He hoped they were safe, and had managed to escape the clutches of those sent for their charge, but he couldn't rely on that.

He regarded King Philip, on his throne, the slight curls at the edges of his mouth suggesting he too was enjoying the show, the three women in custody led around the Court for all to see, their tear-stained cheeks and soiled clothes heartbreaking, even if they were guilty of the crimes of which they were accused. And though they might be, and though they might deserve whatever punishment the Court recommended, his cousin wasn't.

He stepped forward. "I am Sir Marcus de Rancourt, and I ask to be heard on the matter of the charges against Lady Joanne de Rohan."

Silence swept over the massive room, whispers beginning as those who recognized him from several weeks ago made themselves heard.

But it was the King who would decide.

King Philip's eyes flared slightly as he recognized Marcus, a frown spreading momentarily before his displeasure was checked. Marcus had always suspected the King was behind what had happened several weeks ago, at least tacitly, and with his plans thwarted, Marcus had little doubt the monarch wasn't pleased to see him again.

He flicked his wrist, and Marcus bowed. "Thank you, Your Highness. I am not here to address the charges against these women present today, only those against Lady Joanne. I now have proof that she is innocent of all charges."

Gasps filled the room, and the prosecutor who had presented the charges stepped forward, outrage on his face. "And what proof do you have?"

Marcus acknowledged the man with a slight bow. "The body of a woman posing as Lady Joanne, and admission from the man Lady Joanne is accused of having an affair with that he was misled into thinking the dead woman was her."

"Ridiculous! Witnesses have put Lady Joanne with Sir Denys on numerous occasions, and he has even admitted it to others."

"Others who are no doubt here today?"

The man nodded. "Some."

103

Marcus surveyed the room. "And if they took his word that he was having the affair, will they now take his word that he was actually mistaken in her identity?"

Laughter erupted from those gathered, though he noticed a few eyes cast at the floor.

"How, *Sir* Marcus, could that possibly have happened?"

Marcus spun back toward the prosecutor. "Through an elaborate plot that I have only uncovered part of."

The man chuckled, giving an exaggerated sweep of his arm toward those gathered. "Oh, pray, do tell!"

Marcus smiled, taking the insolence as an invitation. "Thank you, I shall." He turned to his audience. "My cousin, through my sister's marriage, Lady Joanne, arrived at my farm yesterday, pursued by men acting on behalf of her husband, Lord Charles. After a *discussion*, they departed, and I agreed to meet with her husband, to discuss the accusations against her, accusations she swore were false."

"As any guilty woman would."

Marcus kept his back to the prosecutor. "Perhaps, but also as any *innocent* woman would. We arrived in Paris last evening, spoke to her husband, and found out the name of the man with whom she was apparently having the affair, Sir Denys de Montfort. We met with him shortly after, and he revealed a portrait of him with his lover, that he was to surprise her with that night. The woman in the portrait was *not* Lady Joanne."

Marcus held up a hand, cutting off the prosecutor before he could interrupt, though he had to wait for the shock to subside upon the members of the Court. "Rest assured, I did consider the possibility that perhaps the artist was simply better suited to another profession, though his likeness of Sir Denys was excellent. This question as to the identity of the woman was enough to convince Sir Denys to let us accompany him to his latest rendezvous with the supposed Lady Joanne. We caught her, and she did indeed match the portrait painted in her honor. We challenged her as to her identity, and she refused to admit the truth. To settle the matter, we took her to meet her so-called husband, Lord Charles, and he confirmed he had never seen this woman before."

Gasps filled the Court, an eruption of angry questions and charges of lies and deceit filled the air for several moments before a raised hand from the King settled them. Marcus continued.

"After interrogating her, she admitted she had been hired to impersonate Lady Joanne, the reason for which I am not yet aware, however I suspect it has something to do with what is going on here today."

The prosecutor chuckled, a mocking smile on his face as he looked at those gathered. "And what would a Templar Knight know of the goings on of the Court?"

Marcus finally acknowledged him. "Enough to smell a set-up when I see one."

Chuckles and more outrage, likely split between those who believed the charges, and those who didn't, spread through the room.

He raised a hand slightly. "I will only say this. Lady Joanne is innocent, as accepted by her husband and her alleged accomplice, and all charges against her should be dropped. And I would suggest, that all charges against these other women be examined carefully, for perhaps they too have been set up like Lady Joanne, in order to embarrass their husbands for some nefarious scheme someone in this Court is fully aware of."

This time the outrage was near universal, the perceived insult to the Court unacceptable among those who held themselves above all others.

Time to leave.

He bowed deeply to King Philip, then spun, marching swiftly from the Court, Simon on his heels. They stepped outside and descended into the courtyard.

"Well, you certainly know how to make an impression."

Marcus chuckled. "Too much?"

Simon shrugged. "Perhaps a little. Soon we won't be welcome there at all."

Marcus grunted. "I can't say that would disappoint me."

106

Enclos du Temple, Templar Fortress
Paris, Kingdom of France

"I'm sorry, but the lady can't stay here."

David frowned, controlling the frustrated anger that threatened to erupt. They had left the farm late in the night, setting up camp outside of Crécy-la-Chapelle until the morning, then made their way to the safest place they could think of, the Templar headquarters for France.

Yet now it might have proven a mistake, Sir Matthew Norris, the Templar Master for France, refusing to let them stay, despite the explanation just given.

"You two, of course, are welcome, but a woman cannot stay here under any circumstances, unless she is a nun."

Jeremy wasn't controlling his emotions as well as David, and he tossed his hands into the air. "But she *must* stay somewhere! She's in danger!"

Sir Matthew nodded at the younger man. "Yes, of course she must. Perhaps the nunnery would have her. It isn't far. You could leave her with them, then return here."

David shook his head. "No, my orders were clear. *We* are to protect her."

"Whose orders?"

"Sir Marcus de Rancourt."

"Ah, Sir Marcus! He's your master?"

"Yes."

107

"Of course, I remember now. He was of some small service a few weeks ago to the Order."

Jeremy continued to spout. "*Small?* He only saved us all!"

Matthew smiled as if dealing with a simpleton. "Of course, though we all have our interpretations of things, don't we?"

David held out a hand, holding Jeremy back.

Matthew ignored the scene. "If Sir Marcus has met with the lady's husband, perhaps he knows how to reach him."

David shook his head, releasing Jeremy as the pressure against his hand subsided. "I'm not sure how wise it would be to let Lord Charles know we are in the city."

Matthew nodded. "True, true, especially with the scandal."

David's eyes narrowed. "What scandal?"

"Arrest warrants were issued for several wives of the Court." Matthew paused, finally looking at Lady Joanne, something he had avoided doing the entire time. "What did you say your name was?"

"Lady Joanne de Rohan."

He shuffled through several papers on his desk, soon finding what he was searching for. "Yes, you are listed. If I were to carry out my duties, I should arrest you now and turn you over to the authorities."

Jeremy reached for his sword, but Matthew waved him off. "But don't worry, I have no intention of doing that. The King's Court is not, shall we say, a place necessarily driven by justice, and from what I've heard here today, perhaps there is reason to question the lady's guilt." He regarded the three of them. "How about we simply say you were never here?"

David bowed deeply. "That would probably be wise."

Matthew clapped his hands together. "Excellent. Provision yourselves from our stores for whatever journey you have, and as I said, the two of you are welcome here at any time, and I'm certain the lady would be at the nunnery as well."

David sighed. "Unfortunately, that's simply not an option. If only there were some other place we could go." He turned to Lady Joanne. "Do you have any friends you could trust?"

She shook her head. "None that I would dare put at risk."

Matthew held up a finger. "Wait, I may have an idea. Was there not a boy involved in the events of a few weeks ago? The son of a forger?"

Jeremy nodded, his eyes widening. "Yes! Thomas!"

"Yes, that was it. If I'm not mistaken, he doesn't live that far from here. When I met with him, he gave me his address. It should be in our files. One moment." Matthew left the room, leaving them to discuss the possibility.

"If Thomas is still living in his father's home, it would at least give us a place to put Lady Joanne where she could be safe," said Jeremy.

David agreed. "Yes, at least until we find Sir Marcus."

The door opened and Matthew returned, holding a piece of paper. He handed it to David. "This is the address, and a quick map on how to get there. It's not a good part of the city, I'm afraid." He gestured at

Lady Joanne. "You might want to change into something less conspicuous."

David regarded her and nodded. "Umm, where could we find women's clothes?"

Matthew shook his head. "Certainly not here, I can assure you. Again, may I suggest the nunnery?"

Palais de la Cité
Paris, Kingdom of France

"Sirs, I would speak with you."

Marcus and Simon turned to see a man following them out of the Court, Marcus noting the cane gripped tightly in the man's left hand. Beyond that one item, however, he bore no resemblance whatsoever to the man he had given chase to, or as had been described by the gatekeeper at the drawbridge. This man was rather short in stature, with a few too many extra pounds packed around his midriff.

And certainly incapable of escaping across a rooftop.

Marcus bowed. "How may we be of assistance?"

"I am Lord Victor de Courtenay. I want to first congratulate you on your success several weeks ago—it was a triumphant moment. I quite enjoyed your display. Should you ever leave the Order, you would make an excellent orator."

Marcus smiled slightly. "I doubt I'll be leaving."

The man chuckled. "Of course, of course. But my purpose for delaying you today, is to let you know that what is happening here is far more dangerous than those previous events. You must be very careful. In fact, I fear for your lives."

Marcus' eyebrows rose slightly. "And why is that?"

"You are not familiar with the Court, are you?"

Marcus shook his head. "Not at all."

"Evidently, or you would not have spoken as you did." Victor lowered his voice, leaning in closer. "All of the women accused are wives to men who favor the truce that currently exists between us and Flanders."

Marcus had no idea of what truce the man was speaking. "So, you are saying these accusations are politically motivated?"

The man nodded vigorously. "Absolutely. Should these men be embarrassed by the alleged actions of their wives, they will lose their influence in the Court, and those they sway. Should that happen, we could return to war, and that could have devastating consequences."

Simon grunted. "Why would anyone want war?"

Victor shrugged. "There are many reasons. Should one be confident one will win, and play a pivotal role, one might seek war to increase one's lands and holdings. While this is possible, it is my belief that something more is going on here."

"What?" asked Marcus.

"I believe a foreign power is at work, seeking to weaken the Kingdom by forcing us into a war that we could lose, or could bankrupt us. Our finances are already on shaky grounds, as I'm sure you are aware. Another war, and it could be the end of us all."

Marcus was aware of some of the money problems due to his involvement in the events of several weeks ago. Apparently, the King owed a massive amount to the Templars and the Jews. "Do you have any idea who it could be?"

Victor shook his head. "Unfortunately, we have many enemies. I frankly have no idea who it could be. But I must warn you. If whoever is behind this is willing to risk war and the lives of thousands, he won't hesitate to eliminate a Templar Knight and his faithful sergeant, should either get in his way."

Marcus frowned. "I will need to think about this. I thank you for the warning, Lord Victor." He motioned toward the cane. "May I ask why you require a cane?"

The man glanced at it, as if he had forgotten he had it. "Do you mean is it an affectation or a necessity?"

Marcus bowed slightly. "Forgive me for asking."

The man chuckled. "No need, my good sir. It is, unfortunately, a necessity. At least for now. Several months ago, there was a terrible accident at the joust in honor of Louis IX's canonization as a saint. The stage holding the King's Court and their guests collapsed, injuring many, including myself. My leg was unfortunately shattered, and the doctor tells me I will likely never walk again without this infernal thing."

Marcus' heart rate ticked up a notch as a thought occurred to him. "I'm sorry to hear that. So, many were injured, some requiring a cane?"

Victor eyed him. "I sense there is a reason for your question, beyond concern for my wellbeing." He held up a hand as Marcus was about to explain. "I won't ask you what, but I will answer your question. Yes, many required canes, and many still do."

Marcus pursed his lips, his mind racing. "Would there be a guest list for this event?"

"For those sitting on that particular stand, absolutely."

Marcus tried to control his excitement at the revelation. "And where might we find such a list?"

The man chuckled. "*You* won't, but I can get it. Meet me at my home tonight. I will have it for you."

Marcus bowed. "Thank you, sir, your assistance is appreciated."

"Think nothing of it. But remember my warning. You are not safe, nor, I fear, am I for speaking with you."

Approaching the Durant Residence
Paris, Kingdom of France

David suppressed a smile at the plain clothes Lady Joanne now wore. Sir Matthew had been right. The nuns had been more than willing to help, and had even provided her with a change of clothing should her exile be longer than hoped. They had also extended an invitation for her to return should shelter not be found.

But as suspected, two men would not be welcome to stay.

David just hoped that not only did Thomas Durant still reside where Sir Matthew had said, but that he'd be willing to take them in. He had only met him once, several weeks ago, and knew nothing about him except that his father had been a forger of some skill, and had been murdered, leaving the young man all alone.

Other than that, and the fact Sir Marcus had extended an invitation to join them on the farm, he knew nothing.

Jeremy pointed ahead. "I think this is it."

David frowned at the sight. If this had ever been a thriving business, it had to have been years ago, if not decades. Though that being said, the entire neighborhood appeared as if a good wind might take it down. He dismounted, tying his horse up, and pointed at Tanya to stay. The dog dropped her hindquarters onto the ground, panting rapidly, excited by the unfamiliar sights and sounds of Paris.

115

David knocked on the door and heard some shuffling inside, but no one answered. He frowned, noting the boards over the windows.

Perhaps he's ignoring everyone.

He knocked again. "Master Thomas, my name is David. I'm a squire to Sir Marcus de Rancourt. We met—"

The door suddenly opened and the young man, appearing gaunt and tired, stared at him wide-eyed. "Come in!" he said, ushering them inside, quickly closing the door behind them. Though it appeared beyond humble from the outside, what David saw inside surprised him. A fire roared to his left, kicking out enough heat to warm the coldest of souls, a healthy-sized bird was roasting at the periphery, and a table was filled with food and drink, a well-dressed though indecently posed woman sitting at it, her legs spread, her mouth full.

"I have a favor to ask of you," said David to Thomas, motioning toward Lady Joanne. "If it wouldn't be too inconvenient, I'd like to leave Lady Joanne here with you, until we find Sir Marcus."

Thomas shrugged, dropping into a chair and tearing off a piece of bread. "I should open a hostel." He gestured at the woman. "Sir Marcus left her here earlier."

Jeremy stepped forward, excitement on his face. "He was here?"

"Yes, only a few hours ago. I assume he'll be back eventually."

David smiled at his partner. "This is good news."

The woman wiped her mouth on her sleeve. "So, you're the lady in question; hey?"

Lady Joanne regarded her. "I'm not sure what you mean."

"Well, they wouldn't tell me names, but you sort of look like Melanie. I don't see why she had to die though for the likes of you."

Joanne's eyes bulged. "I assure you, I have no idea of what you speak!"

"Oh, don't get your knickers in a knot. You're innocent, we all know it. Sir Denys was planting himself in my girl, not you."

Joanne blushed, but moved closer to the woman. "You mean, you know I'm innocent? That I wasn't having an affair?"

"Yes."

"Does my husband know?"

"I should think so."

Joanne spun toward David. "Then I can go home! It's over!"

David shook his head. "I think we should be cautious, Milady. We don't know what's actually happened. I suggest you stay here until we get confirmation from Sir Marcus." He turned to Jeremy. "You stay here with her, and I'll take Tanya to Lord Charles' estate. He might know where we can find Sir Marcus and Simon."

"Sounds good." Jeremy eyed the food. "And smells good." His stomach audibly rumbled, and Thomas chuckled, waving a hand at the spread.

"Please, eat. There's more than enough for a change."

Jeremy leaped at the bird, tearing off a leg then stood at the table, no chairs remaining. David's own stomach demanded attention, and he joined in, deciding a few moments wouldn't change anything.

But not before satisfying an increasingly whining Tanya.

Approaching the de Rohan Residence
Paris, Kingdom of France

Marcus held up a fist, bringing them to a halt as he cocked an ear, listening. He could have sworn he had heard a harsh whisper in the darkness of the alleys surrounding them, the sun low on the horizon, the shadows long and unrevealing.

Something wasn't right.

He had the sense they had been followed for some time, but he had yet to spot anyone, whomever it might be, clearly an expert. Lord Victor had warned them they were in danger, and he had no doubt his warning wasn't paranoia. Whatever was going on was serious. Four wives of prominent members of the King's Court stood accused of heinous crimes, their husband's reputations shattered, and perhaps a foreign government at play, though he had yet to see any evidence to suggest Victor's theory had any validity to it.

But if it did, then a Templar Knight and his sergeant would surely be forfeit if they threatened the plans of those who would involve themselves in such devious undertakings.

A sword drew from a scabbard in an alley to their right, confirming his suspicions. He drew his own, turning to engage the hidden enemy, Simon facing his horse in the opposite direction to cover their rear.

"And here I thought our pleasant day would end uneventfully."

Marcus grunted. "Unfortunately, someone has different plans for us." He glanced to his right, two men stepping from the shadows and into the street they had just passed. "I've got two on my right."

"And I have two on *my* right. Looks like we're fighting."

Marcus listened, and two more came from the alleyway he now faced. "It looks that way." His horse suddenly cried out, rearing up on its hind legs and tossing him from the saddle. It struggled forward several steps before its hindquarters gave out, an arrow embedded deep into the muscle. Simon's steed whinnied in agony a moment later as an arrow pierced its neck, Simon jumping clear before it collapsed and crushed him.

"Looks like we're on our feet then." Marcus surged toward the alley, swinging his sword at the two blocking his path as he tried to escape the aim of the archer who had forced them to their feet. His blow was parried, as was his second, the man evidently skilled, though this fact failed to concern Marcus.

The Lord was on his side, and should he lose, his afterlife was secured.

He parried his opponent's swing and advanced, grabbing the man's arm and yanking him forward, plunging his sword into the man's belly before kicking him off the blade. Simon was already battling the second man, and the fact the archer hadn't taken either of them out of the battle suggested, at least for the moment, he had no angle.

Simon swung his sword upward from the right, carrying his opponent's blade high and away, exposing his side. Marcus swung, cleaving a deep gash into the man's torso, then spun toward the front of the alley, four more now silhouetted in the fading light.

An arrow zipped past Marcus' ear and he glanced up, an archer now visible across the street, standing in plain view, knowing they had no way to challenge him. Marcus glanced around them, finding nowhere to hide, the darkness in which they found themselves the only thing saving them now.

But the archer would eventually find his mark, and if he didn't, his friends would likely best at least one of them.

The archer cried out and fell from the roof, gripping his side, his compatriots spinning to witness his body slam into the cobblestone. One of the men cried out, an arrow visible in his neck, and Marcus smiled, thanking the good Lord for sending assistance, whoever it might be.

"Shall we?"

Simon grunted. "I thought you'd never ask."

Marcus surged forward, Simon at his side, as their opponents, now only three, split their attention between them and the new arrival. A dog snarled, leaping into view, and Marcus smiled as he recognized Tanya. He lunged forward, dropping close to the ground as he swung low, removing the man's leg below the knee, as Simon pressed forward, piercing the chest of his man. Another, occupied by Tanya's jaws, dropped from an arrow.

And then there were none.

Tanya was still yanking at her moaning opponent, threatening to tear his arm off.

Marcus saved him from any further suffering. "Tanya, sit!"

The dog immediately obeyed its master, and the man she had been holding scrambled away, helping his one-legged comrade down the street, the rest dead or dying. David emerged from around the corner, a smile on his face.

Marcus kneeled to give Tanya a good scratch. "What are you doing here?"

"Saving your asses, apparently."

Simon stared at one of those he had bested, the last gurgles of life heard. "I think we were just about to get the upper hand."

"Of course you were."

Marcus slapped David on the back. "I'm glad you showed up when you did. That archer almost had us." He frowned. "But where is Lady Joanne? Is she safe?"

"Yes, she's with Jeremy at Thomas Durant's home."

Marcus chuckled. "I'm happy to hear it. I assume there was a problem?"

"Yes. Several of the King's guard came to arrest her. They tried to rape her, but we fought them off. I felt it was best to leave the farm, just in case."

"The children?"

"They're fine. I had sent them to stay with Isabelle and her mother, just in case anything happened."

"Good thinking."

David cursed. "Maybe not."

"What?"

"I didn't tell her we were leaving."

Simon groaned. "There'll be no living with her now."

Marcus chuckled. "I'm sending you back first."

122

"What did I ever do to you?"

"I'm sure I'll think of something."

David brought them back to the moment. "Lady Joanne asked of her husband. She wondered if it were safe for her to return."

Marcus shook his head. "No, I don't believe so. At the moment, her arrest warrant is probably still valid, and we don't know yet who wishes her and her husband harm." He motioned at Tanya. "Take her back to Thomas', and protect Lady Joanne and Mrs. Thibault. We'll be back as soon as we can."

"Yes, sir."

Durant Residence
Paris, Kingdom of France

"I find that interesting."

Thomas Durant eyed the wine sitting on the floor beside him, the feast having moved to a blanket laid out before the fire, now that there were four of them and only two chairs left. Mrs. Thibault had been pestering him with questions, and had just learned that not only did he know how to read and write, his late father was a forger.

The non-stop interrogation was giving him the urge to down every drop of alcohol within reach, then seek out more.

But that wouldn't solve his problems.

"Wait a moment. Durant! Is your father Max Durant?"

His chest ached at the mention of his father, and by someone as loathsome as this woman. He nodded.

"Oh, he had skills, let me tell you. You should be proud to be his son. I employed him on many an occasion. He spoke of you often. Very proud indeed."

Thomas stared at her as her words sank in. "You knew my father?"

"Yes! Why, we were practically friends, at least as close a friend as business relations can be. My late husband especially took a liking to him, using him whenever he could. I guess you could say I continued the tradition." She wagged a finger at him. "Never let someone get away who has skills you might need."

She winked at Lady Joanne. "And a tight tongue!" She howled with laughter, and Thomas and Joanne exchanged an awkward glance.

Thibault finally settled down, taking a drink of her wine. "So, do you have any of his skills?"

Thomas shook his head. "Just reading and writing."

"So, you're not an expert forger like your father?"

"I could never draw a steady line. I guess I took after my mother."

The woman nodded, scratching under her armpit. "No shame in that, boy. Reading and writing is no small thing in these parts. Tell me, how did you feel about your father's line of work? I mean, being a criminal and all?"

Thomas' chest tightened, and a surge of anger rushed through him at her words, but she was right. He *was* a criminal. And it was what had got him killed. He inhaled slowly, calming himself. "He did what was necessary to provide for his family."

"And you didn't mind that he was a criminal?"

"I would rather he not have been, but I loved my father, and I miss him dearly. I won't have anyone speak ill of him."

Thibault leaned over and patted him on the leg. "Of course, dear." She paused, eying him for a moment. "You know, a young man of your skills could go far if he were willing to bend a rule or two."

"And break a lot more," said Sir Marcus' squire, Jeremy. He gestured toward Thibault while leaning closer to Thomas. "Be careful with this one, Master Thomas. I have a feeling she isn't the sort your late parents would want you consorting with."

"Yes," added Joanne. "Leave the poor boy alone. You're a terrible influence."

Thibault frowned, turning her attention to the only lady in the room. "You barely know me, yet you judge me."

"I know the type."

Thibault chuckled. "I doubt it, Milady. The likes of me rarely frequent the ivory towers the likes of you call home."

"I'd hardly call it an ivory tower."

Thibault waved her hand at their surroundings. "Compared to this, I think any in this neighborhood would."

Joanne frowned, dipping her head slightly. "I will give you that."

"As you should. When you grow up orphaned in these parts, you find you sometimes are forced to do things you never thought possible." Thibault sighed. "My late husband and I had no parents. It was how we met. We became a team, picking the pockets of the rich when we had the opportunity. It kept us fed and warm enough. As we got older, my husband organized the street children, and we made a good life for ourselves and the little ones."

Joanne grunted. "It sounds like you exploited the desperate souls of these cursed parts."

"Aye, for their benefit and mine, I assure you. Exploitation is good, if at least someone benefits. We never robbed from the poor—the poor have nothing to steal! We only took from those who could afford to give, should they have been charitable souls. But most of those with means that you find in these parts are either criminals themselves, or here to truly exploit.

You would be shocked at the depravity of some of those I have encountered, that you probably consort with in the King's Court."

Joanne stared at her skeptically. "I doubt that."

Thibault smiled. "Yet here you are, in hiding because those very people have implicated you in a heinous crime that you are innocent of."

Joanne's head drooped and her shoulders sagged in defeat. "You're right, of course. I guess I shouldn't judge what I don't understand."

Thibault patted Joanne's knee, her voice becoming gentler. "No, you shouldn't, dear, but we're all guilty of it from time to time." She pointed at Thomas. "Take this boy. I could put him to work tomorrow. I have need of someone who can read and write—they are so rare in these parts. He could be making more money in a day than he probably has earned in weeks lying about here, feeling sorry for himself." She reached out and grabbed his arm. "What do you say, boy? Would you like to come work for me? Lift yourself out of this wretched life you've found yourself trapped in?"

The door swung open, David and the dog entering with a blast of frigid air. He closed the door, stomping his feet to warm himself, the distraction saving Thomas from a difficult discussion.

Joanne eagerly turned toward the new arrival. "Do you have news?"

David nodded, taking a seat close to the fire, Tanya lying down beside him, her snout working hard at drawing every scent wafting from the food laid out before them. "I found Sir Marcus and Simon. It is Sir Marcus' opinion that you should remain here.

Although your husband knows you are innocent in this affair, Sir Marcus feels it isn't safe enough yet for you to travel."

Thibault cleared her throat. "And am I to remain here as well?"

David reached for a piece of bread. "Yes, both of you are. When I found them, they were being set upon by at least seven men. They barely escaped with their lives. And if they aren't safe, then none of us are."

De Rohan Residence
Paris, Kingdom of France

"I understand you arrived without horses."

Marcus bowed as Lord Charles de Rohan entered the room, Simon doing the same. "Yes, Milord, this is true. We were accosted on our way here by seven men. They targeted our horses to get us on the ground."

Charles' eyes examined them both. "You seem unscathed."

"We were fortunate they weren't as skilled as us, Milord."

"Evidently." He sat behind his desk, not offering them chairs. "You have news?"

"Yes, sir, much has happened today. After I received your message last night, I sent word to my squires to move your wife to safety. I have heard from them, and she is indeed safe."

"And where is she? Shouldn't she return here?"

Marcus shook his head. "No, sir, as we were just attacked very near here, I feel it isn't safe yet for her to return home, however, I'm certain she is relieved to know you no longer think her guilty."

Charles grunted. "Yes, of course. I just would feel better with her here, where I can protect her."

"I understand your feelings on the matter, however I ask that you trust me with her safety."

"Yet here you stand."

Marcus bowed slightly. "Yes, but she is with trusted men, skilled in battle. She will be safe." Marcus continued with his update. "We found the residence of the now deceased imposter, Miss Girard. We found little of interest, except where she had been hired, though discovered little of value, as the man she met disguised himself. We returned to the coachman's, only to discover him dead in his room, visited earlier by a man who again disguised himself."

"I'm sensing a theme."

"Yes, sir, unfortunately. We then found the woman who hired them both, as she was being attacked by whom we believe to be the same man."

"Is she all right?"

"Yes. We've moved her somewhere safe until this matter is closed."

"Where? With my wife?"

"I think it's best we keep these things to ourselves, in case anyone might be listening."

Charles frowned, but flicked a hand, signaling Marcus to continue.

"We went to the Court to hear the charges read against your wife and the others, and I spoke on her behalf. I'm not sure if it carried any weight, yet it should be enough to at least cast some doubt on her guilt, perhaps long enough to stem the damage to your reputation, and hers."

"Anything else?"

"No." Marcus felt a twinge of guilt, as it was a lie, though a necessary one. He had failed to mention anything said by Lord Victor, this the only hope he still had of making progress in his inquiries.

"So, what do we do next?" asked Charles, clearly not pleased with the progress.

"I'm afraid we're at a bit of an impasse. Whoever is behind this, has killed all of the witnesses we're aware of."

Simon cleared his throat. "Umm, there's still one."

Marcus and Charles looked at him. "Who?" asked Charles.

Simon bowed slightly. "Umm, sir, Milord, there's whoever delivered the message yesterday morning, telling of the lady's crimes."

Marcus' eyebrows rose. "That's right. Somebody had to deliver it, though I doubt that will lead to anyone. Even if we could find out who did deliver the message, they were probably paid in secret by a man wearing a hooded robe."

Simon shrugged. "Probably, but it's all we've got."

"Agreed." Marcus turned to Charles. "We must see the chambermaid, at once."

He frowned, but rose. "Of course." He led them down a series of hallways then into the servants' wing. "I gave her some time to recover from her ordeal. She is free to continue her duties when her mistress returns." He pointed at a door, a guard standing to one side. "Open it."

The guard complied, and they entered to find a young woman sitting on the edge of her bed, her cheeks red and her right eye swollen where she had been recently struck.

She leaped to her feet at the appearance of her master, cowering with a dropped chin and rounded shoulders.

"These men have questions for you."

131

"Y-yes, sir."

Marcus stepped forward, making a point to keep his voice as gentle as possible, the woman clearly having been through an ordeal. "Beatrice, is it?"

The woman nodded.

"I am Sir Marcus de Rancourt. Your mistress is my cousin through marriage. My sister married Sir Henri de Foix, your mistress' cousin."

Her eyes widened. "Then she found him!"

"No, I'm afraid Sir Henri is dead some two years, but she did find me, and is now safe."

"Where?"

"That is unimportant. I assure you where she is, no one will find her."

Beatrice stole a glance at her master, standing at the door. "That-that is good. I have been worried about her."

"No doubt. But in order to help her, I need one question answered."

"Yes?"

"How did you obtain the note that was left for your master, telling the falsehoods of your mistress' adultery?"

Her mouth opened to answer, then she hesitated, her eyes narrowing in confusion. "I-I can't remember! I mean, I didn't find it, it was given to me."

"By whom?"

Beatrice grabbed the top of her head, squeezing her arms tight against the sides, moaning. She finally let go, lifting her chin. "Albert, the stable boy, perhaps?" She threw her hands up. "I'm sorry, it's all a blur! Everything that happened yesterday is so muddled, I-I really can't say for certain. I know it was one of the staff, and I know I met with Albert, because, well, I asked him to help my mistress, umm, escape." She glanced over at her master, still terrified.

Charles raised a hand, a slight smile on his face. "It's all right, all is forgiven."

Her tense shoulders relaxed. "Thank you, Milord." She turned back to Marcus, slightly more at ease. "I'm sorry, sir, but the stable boy is the only person I remember from yesterday morning. I can't say for sure it was him, but it must have been. Surely I'd remember if it weren't, wouldn't I?"

Marcus smiled. "One can never be certain in the heat of the moment what one will remember when things are once again calm." He turned to Charles. "Where can we find this stable boy?"

"I should think the stables."

Marcus smiled at the veiled insult. "Then, please, show us the way. Perhaps he holds the answer we seek."

Palais de la Cité
Paris, Kingdom of France

Lord Victor de Courtenay hurried from the clerk's office, the guest list for the jousting competition tucked neatly inside his tunic. Acquiring the list hadn't been hard, only a few coins needed to expedite the process and assure secrecy. He was certain the Templar Knight that had requested it, suspected that the name of the man behind the unfolding scandal was on it, and he tended to agree it was a possibility.

It had all been prompted by his own cane, which could only mean they suspected someone of being involved who also required one.

And the list definitely contained many who did.

Since their conversation earlier in the day, he had found himself regarding anyone employing a cane with suspicion, and it had left him on edge for too many exhausting hours.

But now he had the list, and a short ride home would have it out of his hands, and into those of Sir Marcus.

His horse was brought to him, and he dismissed the boy as several colleagues from the Court approached. With the horse between them, he noted the ambassador had an ornate cane, and remembered he had been at the games.

It sent his heart racing.

He tucked the pages containing the list underneath the saddle, his horse protesting for a moment, then stepped out into plain view. "Mr. Ambassador, a pleasant day, is it not?"

The ambassador smiled and bowed. "It is that, isn't it? Lord Victor, I would speak to you about your conversation with the Templar Knight that injected himself into the Court's affairs earlier today. Sir Marcus, I believe?"

Victor nodded, tensing. "Yes, I believe that was his name."

"What business did you have with him?"

Victor smiled pleasantly. "I hardly think it is any of your concern, though there's no harm in telling you. I merely wished to congratulate him on his actions of several weeks ago."

"Ahh, yes, it was quite the scandal, was it not? The Court has spoken of little else until today."

Victor chuckled. "Too true, too true." He made to round his horse. "This has been pleasant, my good sir, however I must beg my leave of you, as I have an impatient wife who I *know* has been faithful to me."

The ambassador laughed, then held out a hand, taking Victor by the shoulder. "And what of your business with the clerk?"

Victor's heart pounded as the ambassador's two companions stepped closer. "Now I *know* that is none of your concern." He stared down at the hand. "I'll ask you to unhand me, sir."

The ambassador smiled, then abruptly removed his hand, taking a step back. "I believe you are up to something, sir, something that you should have left alone."

Victor knew this was it, that his time on this earth was done, but he was determined his death would not

135

be in vain. He smacked his horse on the hindquarters, and it whinnied in surprise then bolted. He turned to face his accosters, drawing his sword.

The ambassador smiled. "I accept your challenge." He motioned to his companions. "And so do they."

De Rohan Residence
Paris, Kingdom of France

"Albert, these men have questions for you."

The young man lurched forward, his shoulders rounded, his head down, as he avoided eye contact with his master. "Y-Yes, sir."

"And when they're done, prepare two horses for them. They're in need."

"Y-Yes, sir, I-I'll try to find some."

"Don't try, my boy, do!"

"Y-Yes, sir."

Marcus bowed slightly at Charles. "Thank you for your generosity, Milord. We'll have them returned once we resupply at a Templar post."

"Of course, of course."

Marcus turned to Albert, the stable boy. "You know Beatrice, your mistress' chambermaid?"

Albert's cheeks flushed, and he giggled. "Umm, yes?"

"She says you gave her a letter yesterday morning, and told her it was for your master."

Albert rapidly shook his head. "Oh, no, I gave her no such letter." He paused, his eyes darting toward Charles. "I, umm, well, she umm, did come to see me about a horse for Lady Joanne. She, umm, asked me to keep it quiet." His head spun toward Charles, his eyes wide with terror and tears. "I-I didn't want to, sir, but she said it was approved by you, but that I

137

shouldn't tell you if asked. It confused me, sir! I-I'm sorry if I failed you." His shoulders slumped.

Charles patted him on the back. "You didn't, my boy. You should always provide for your mistress' safety. But you say there was no note?"

Albert shook his head. "No, sir, none." He glanced at Marcus. "But I'm rarely near the gate. Perhaps someone else? Perhaps she's simply confused? She did seem in quite the state."

Charles frowned. "Very well. Thank you, Albert. Now see to those horses."

"Y-Yes, sir." Albert bolted.

Marcus turned to Charles. "I think it's time we gathered your entire staff and ask them directly, rather than do this one at a time."

Charles nodded, though reluctantly. Marcus could understand the man's hesitation. There was little doubt the entire household knew what had happened, and of what his wife was accused.

And it had to be embarrassing.

Though from his experience, those in positions like Lord Charles, rarely cared what those beneath them thought.

De Courtenay Residence
Paris, Kingdom of France

"Something's wrong!"

Gerard stopped what he was doing, brush in midair as he held the lead for one of the master's many fine horses. The ado was coming from the main gate to the estate, and he hurried to return the massive beast to its stall so he could see what was happening.

"Get the mistress!"

His eyes bulged. Though he was still young, in all his years, he had never heard the lady of the house called for in such a panic.

Something truly horrible must be going on.

He slapped the horse gently on the hindquarters, and it hurried forward the final few steps into the stall. He yanked it closed, making sure it was locked, then sprinted toward the courtyard, his eyes wide with excitement, hoping he hadn't missed whatever was transpiring.

As he came out into the failing light of the early evening, he skidded to a halt, spotting a number of the staff gathered around the master's horse.

What are they all excited about?

The mistress rushed down the steps, accompanied by her entourage, her face one of business, and he had to admit it was odd to see her at this hour. The master usually came home around now from the palace, and she'd be inside preparing for dinner. Their greetings never took place outside.

139

The master!

Lord Victor wasn't among those gathered around the horse. He squinted as he struggled to see him through the crowd, and as it parted for the mistress, he was sure he wasn't there.

Then where is he?

"It arrived like this?" demanded the mistress.

"Yes, Milady. Without a rider."

She pointed at someone. "Send a runner to the Court to check on my husband. And bring a spare horse. I'm sure this one simply got away and made her way here. No need to panic. She's made the ride thousands of times and knows her way." She gave the steed a gentle pat on the neck. "Now everyone, back to work, we won't worry until there's something to worry about!"

The crowd broke, and somebody sprinted past him for the stables, no doubt the runner ordered. He stepped forward and took the lead of his master's horse from one of the guards, and led her back to the stable, noticing her nose kept turning to the left, as if she were trying to scratch herself where the saddle was.

"What is it, girl, is something bothering you?"

The horse snorted as they entered the stable. He tied her lead to a post, then proceeded to remove the saddle. A bundle of papers fell to the ground.

"What's this?" He picked up the pages, staring at what was written on them, the two columns of letters on each page nothing but chicken scratches to him. "Did someone stick this under your saddle? No wonder you ran away. The bastards." He tossed the pages into the corner, cursing, the horse snorting with what sounded to him to be satisfaction.

He proceeded to brush her down, paying particular attention to the area where the papers had irritated her. "There, there, girl, you're all right now. We'll get you all settled, and you'll be all better in no time."

He glanced at the papers in the corner as the runner left with two horses, the question of what had happened to his master forgotten.

Who would do such a thing?

De Rohan Residence
Paris, Kingdom of France

"And nobody remembers giving a message to Beatrice?"

Heads shook once again as Marcus repeated the question. None of the gathered staff were admitting to passing on the message, and apparently, with the exception of the chambermaid, Beatrice, all were present.

He sighed. "Does anyone remember seeing Beatrice, at least?"

The stable boy, Albert, raised his hand.

Then finally another. "I saw her go into the master's study, sir, just after I delivered his breakfast."

Charles pursed his lips, nodding. "Yes, I found the message under the tray when I pushed it aside. I think she meant to delay me finding out about the accusations." Drawing in a deep breath that swelled his chest, he raised his voice. "Accusations, I might add, which have been proven false, no matter what you have heard."

The same woman bowed her head. "We never doubted it, Milord. The mistress loves you very much."

Charles bowed slightly. "And I her, but that is none of your concern." He smiled. "Though your acknowledgment is appreciated."

She blushed and curtsied.

"If anyone remembers anything, please come see me immediately. We must find out who delivered this note." He waved a hand. "Dismissed."

The staff quickly broke, returning to their duties as Marcus, Simon, and Charles conferred.

"I don't understand," said Charles. "Someone must have given her the note."

Marcus agreed. "Either one of your staff is lying, or someone came onto the property and gave it to the chambermaid, then left."

Charles nodded. "That is definitely possible. Tradesmen pass through and deliveries are made constantly. During the day, the gate is merely for show. We have no enemies here, and the guards merely ask what business someone has, and they let them through if the answer is reasonable." He sighed. "I think we'll have to tighten up security around here when this is done."

Marcus shook his head. "I would do so immediately. Something is going on, and I fear for your safety."

Charles frowned. "You might be right. I'll take care of it at once."

The man left, heading for the gate, and Marcus stared at the sun, low on the horizon. "We should make our way to Lord Victor's now. This business took longer than I expected, and we're late."

"Perhaps we'll be in time for dinner?"

Marcus chuckled as they headed for the stables. "Something tells me we wouldn't be welcome at the table of a Lord."

"I bathed just yesterday. And I promise to be on my best behavior."

Marcus eyed his sergeant. "Have you ever noticed how when you're hungry, everyone sits at least an arm's length away from you when you're eating. You're like a beast!"

Simon grinned. "I do love my food!"

"I think we'll have to wait until we return to Master Thomas'."

"Are we spending the night?"

"I think we should. I don't trust Mrs. Thibault enough to leave them all alone with her."

De Courtenay Residence
Paris, Kingdom of France

Gerard watched, shocked, as this time the entire household gathered, the courtyard full as word of Lord Victor's murder spread. The runner had returned only moments ago, crying out the news as he raced up to the grounds and through the gates. The mistress had heard from inside, and rushed onto the steps, collapsing at the news.

It was horrifying, and his jaw hadn't closed since he had first comprehended the news.

Wails filled the air, renewed as a cart arrived a short while later carrying the body of the master. The mistress, recovered only moments before, collapsed again on her husband's body, sobbing in agony, brushing off the staff who tried to pull her away.

Gerard wasn't sure what he was supposed to do, and was doubly troubled when two Templars rode through the gates, one a knight in his bright white surcoat with red cross, the other a sergeant, his surcoat black.

"What has happened here?" demanded the knight as he dismounted. He approached the cart with the master's body. "Is that Lord Victor?"

"Yes it is," replied someone in the throng. "He's been murdered!"

"By whom?"

The runner sent to find the master earlier, stepped forward. "They don't know."

The mistress rose, wiping the tears from her face and fixing herself before turning to address the new arrivals. "What business do you have here?"

"Milady, I am Sir Marcus de Rancourt. We were to meet with your husband about a matter tonight."

"I sense from your tone that you aren't surprised at this turn of events."

The knight bowed slightly. "Frankly, Milady, it is what I feared might happen."

"Then this matter was dangerous?"

"Yes. Your husband approached us earlier today to warn of the danger, and offered his assistance in obtaining some information that may prove critical in a matter we are looking into."

"What was he supposed to have obtained for you?"

"A list of names."

Gerard paused.

A list!

He thought back to the papers he had found stuck behind the master's saddle. Though he couldn't read the words, he at least recognized that it was a list of something, as opposed to some letter. He rushed into the stables, looking about for the pages he had discarded, and found them amid a pile of hay. He grabbed them, searching through the pile to make certain he had them all, then rushed outside as the Templars appeared to be leaving.

Gerard waved the pages over his head. "Milady, could this be what they were looking for?" He held out the pages as he approached, hunched over, trying unsuccessfully to mix bowing with running.

"What's this?" she asked.

"I'm not sure, ma'am, but I found the pages stuffed under the saddle on the master's horse."

She glared at him. "Why didn't you bring this to me?"

He cowered. "I-I didn't realize it was important."

She swatted him with the pages, then stepped toward the Templars. "This would appear to be a list of names. Could this be what he was getting for you?"

The knight took the pages, nodding as a smile slowly spread before it was checked on the solemnness of the occasion. "It is indeed. Your husband has done us a great service, and I regret he died because of it. Whoever is behind it, however, has made an enemy today, and I intend to bring them to justice, as they are obviously involved in the same situation I am already investigating. You will hear from me soon, Milady."

"I wish you God's speed, Sir Marcus."

The Templars left and the gates closed. Gerard turned toward his mistress, a smile on his face as he realized he had done a good deed.

She smacked him across the cheek. "The next time you find papers, you bring them to me!"

His cheeks burned and his eyes teared. "I-I'm sorry, Milady!"

She collapsed again, two of the staff catching her, and he realized she wasn't truly angry with him, she was simply overwhelmed with everything that had happened. He wiped his eyes dry on the back of his hands, then turned away to give her some privacy, instead staring at the body of his master, and wondered what would now become of them all with no male heir in the household.

En route to Durant Residence
Paris, Kingdom of France

Marcus felt uneasy as they rode for Thomas Durant's home. The list was stuffed under his chainmail, and he'd die before he let anyone get their hands on it, for it was obviously important. Clearly, someone had seen Lord Victor speaking with them, but he couldn't believe that alone would be enough for anyone to want to kill him.

They were merely words.

But the list was evidence, and until the moment he had learned of Victor's death, he hadn't been sure the names on the pages would be of any importance.

Yet clearly they were to someone, and if he gambled, he'd put money on whoever that was, being included in the names.

And he'd also bet that when they didn't discover the list on Victor's person after killing him, they would realize it must have been on his horse, the brave soul obviously having hidden it there before he was attacked.

And if he were the murderer, he would have had someone watching Victor's estate to see who showed up to collect the list.

Then pursue them.

So far, he hadn't been able to spot anyone following them as they rushed through the streets of Paris as quickly and safely as they could, though with the number of people and horses about, it was

149

difficult to say for certain. And as the darkness grew, it only made things more difficult.

As they left the regal estates of the members of the Court and foreign ambassadors, and entered the less desirable area of the grand city where Thomas Durant lived, the numbers on horseback dwindled, most in these parts unable to afford the luxury. And the fact they weren't the only riders, had him slightly uncomfortable.

"There it is," said Simon.

"Keep riding. If we're being followed, I don't want them to know where we're going."

They continued past the dilapidated building, fire and candlelight blaring through the cracks in the boards indicating someone was inside, their numbers concealed. He peered into the darkness ahead. "That alley to the right. Let's head down there."

Simon grunted, leading the way as they turned sharply down the laneway. They galloped toward the end, and Marcus glanced over his shoulder to see two riders follow them.

He suppressed a curse.

Simon didn't.

"Challenge or evade?" asked his sergeant.

"I'm tempted to challenge. Split up at the end of the alley and dismount. We'll surprise them as they come through."

"Good. I'm tired of running."

Simon broke left and Marcus right. He pulled up on his reins and hopped off his horse, drawing his sword and positioning himself at the corner, readying his weapon, Simon doing the same across from him. The sound of the two horses pounding toward them filled his ears, and Marcus steadied his breathing, readying himself for what was to come, for the initial blow would be critical.

The nose of the horse came into sight, the beast's head turning toward him. He smiled as he thrust upward, catching its rider unawares, his arm raised high, sword in hand. Marcus plunged the blade deep, and the rider cried out in agony, the horse rearing on its hind legs in panic. He stepped forward, shoving hard with both hands, lifting the rider from his saddle and into the air before his heart was pierced, and blood flowed freely down the blade and onto Marcus' hands. He stepped back, withdrawing the blade as he checked on his sergeant, his foe leaning far back in his saddle, his head nearly cleaved clean off.

Marcus smiled. "I think our work here is done. Search them. See if you can find anything that might identify who they are, or who they're working for." He pulled his man off his horse, and first searched the saddle for anything, finding nothing but provisions. He then checked the body, finding only a small purse. He took it with the thought of giving it to young Thomas to help him get back on his feet.

He glanced over at Simon. "Anything?" Simon tossed him another purse. "Just this. No papers or accouterments."

"Very well. Let's get out of here before we draw too much attention. And remove your surcoat." Marcus removed his own, rolling it up and shoving it in the saddlebag of his horse, Simon doing the same. They both mounted their steeds, heading quickly down the back alley that Marcus assumed would lead toward Thomas' home.

It took only a short while to find their destination. They tied up the horses and entered through the back, finding everyone in the front of the building that had once been Thomas' late father's workshop. A feast was underway, and Marcus' stomach growled at the sights and smells.

"Sir!" Jeremy leaped to his feet, David following a moment later. "Thank God you are well. Your horses?"

Marcus jerked a thumb over his shoulder. "In the back. Any problems?"

"Nothing."

"Very well. Tend to them, but first get this off me." He held out his arms, as did Simon, his squires quickly freeing them of their armor. It was a glorious feeling that always made him feel light on his feet, as if he could fly, though the sensation only lasted for a few moments before he felt vulnerable.

"I'll tend to the horses," said Jeremy, disappearing in the back. Marcus sat on a blanket, one of several laid out before the roaring fire, the warmth attacking the chill as he surveyed the semi-circle of those now under his protection. It was an odd collection. A criminal pretending to be high-society, an actual noblewoman, the son of a forger, and several Templars.

"We are quite the sight, aren't we!" said Thibault, laughter filling the room with her comment.

Marcus smiled, the wine apparently flowing along with the food laid out in front of everyone. He frowned at the offerings. "I thought I said to keep a low profile."

"We did!" replied Thibault. "Thomas and the squires made several trips and came in through the back. Nobody suspects anything, I assure you."

"Uh huh." He grabbed a leg off a bird roasted to perfection, tearing it away from the carcass, and took a bite as David poured him and Simon wine.

Lady Joanne leaned forward. "What have you found out?"

Marcus swallowed. "Milady, a great deal has happened today, as well as another tragedy. Do you know Lord Victor de Courtenay?"

She nodded. "I do, from the Court. Not well, mind you, though I have exchanged pleasantries. I rarely go, and haven't been in such a long time. I simply can't bear the gossip." She frowned. "I was a great admirer of his wife, Lady—." Her jaw dropped. "Wait. Why? Oh no, please not him!"

"I'm afraid so, Milady. After I addressed the Court on your behalf, he followed us into the palace courtyard and provided us his theory of what may be going on. He promised a list of names at my request, and when we went to his residence to collect, we found that he had been murdered. We feared all was lost, but the good man fulfilled his promise." Marcus retrieved the pages, holding them up in triumph. "He managed to somehow trick his accosters, hiding the pages beneath the saddle of his horse, which in its master's absence, returned home on its own."

Thibault leaned closer, eying the pages. "Whose names are they?"

"I have a theory, furthered when I noticed Lord Victor made use of a cane. He explained that several months earlier, the royal stage at the Louis IX celebrations collapsed, and many were injured."

Joanne's head bobbed. "Yes! This is true. Even my husband hurt his knee quite badly. It took weeks to heal, and it still bothers him to this day."

Marcus exchanged a glance with Simon, then scanned the list carefully for the first time, spotting Lord Charles' name on the second page. "Indeed, he is listed."

"Yes. Many were injured, especially those in the back rows, higher from the ground."

Marcus handed Joanne the list. "Do any names stand out to you?"

She quickly read through them, nodding slowly. "I'm afraid, no. I recognize almost all the names, therefore none really seem unusual."

"Any enemies of your husband?"

"I can't think why he would have any."

"Your husband is a supporter of the truce with Flanders?"

She paused. "Why, I'm not sure. I think so. Isn't everyone?"

Marcus shook his head. "Apparently not."

She sighed. "Politics were never my concern—I left that to my husband, which is why I avoided the Court."

Simon grunted. "That might be why Sir Denys didn't realize the woman he was with wasn't you."

Her eyes widened slightly. "This is true. I've never met the man, and he's rather young, isn't he? He's likely new to the Court." She waved a hand. "I really don't know about these things. My husband and his

154

friends would debate long into the night, and sometimes I would awake to find them still at it in the morning, especially surrounding the war with Flanders and their ally, England. I should think it would have been a great relief to everyone that a truce was signed and so many lives saved."

Marcus agreed. "One would think, however apparently not everyone agreed with the truce."

"Really?"

"Yes. According to Lord Victor, all of those whose wives were accused of adultery today, including your husband, were supporters of the treaty. It was his belief that they were being embarrassed, so that they would lose support in the Court, and traction might be gained to rescind the truce."

Joanne's eyes shot wide. "But that would mean war!"

"Exactly."

"But who would profit from that?" asked David. "Surely if the King wanted war, he would simply declare it."

Joanne nodded. "Yes, and the Court couldn't stop him. And even if he wanted their support, he'd simply have to indicate his desire, and the Court would fall in line, demanding war."

Marcus agreed. "Which is what makes this so puzzling. If the King isn't behind this, then who is, and why?"

"Flanders?" suggested Simon.

Thibault shook her head. "I doubt it. We trounced them quite handily." She shrugged. "Or so I heard."

Joanne looked at her. "I didn't know you followed politics."

"Of course you didn't! You didn't meet me until today. If one wants to profit from the misery of others, one needs to know everything that is going on that could cause misery. Nothing more than war causes misery, and a good *denier* is to be had for those who pay attention to affairs such as this."

Marcus' eyebrows rose. "Speaking of, I almost forgot." He removed the two purses taken from their pursuers. "We took these off the two who followed us here."

Joanne stared at him. "You were followed?"

"Yes."

"And they just let you take their purses?"

Simon chuckled. "After they were dead on the ground."

Joanne gasped at the revelation, while Thibault reached for more wine.

Marcus shook the purses. "I was thinking their contents might prove useful to young Thomas here, to help him through these hard times."

Thomas eyed the purses. "Surely you should keep them, sir. After all, it was you who fought and won."

Marcus smiled at the lad, apparently not a greedy bone to be had in his body. "Actually, as a Templar, I'm forbidden to carry more than four *deniers* on my person at any time, unless on official business." He emptied the contents from one of the purses into his hand, revealing almost a dozen silver coins. "And as you can see, this is far more than a knight sworn to poverty would ever need." Something caught his eye. He picked out one of the coins and held it up to the firelight. "This is odd." He tossed it to Simon. "Tell me what you see."

"A very fine meal, is what I see." He held it up and turned to put the fire behind him. "Who is that?" He handed the coin to Jeremy, he and David examining it.

"There's some writing around the edges," said Jeremy, squinting.

Thomas held out his hand. "May I?"

Jeremy handed it to Thomas who then rose, retrieving a magnifying glass from one of the drawers of the desk his father used to work at. He returned, sitting cross-legged. "It's clearly King Adolf, it says so below his portrait."

Simon shrugged. "So?"

Thibault huffed. "So? They don't make these sergeants too smart, do they?"

Simon growled slightly at her and Marcus held him back with a smile. "Fine, oh wise one, what is so important about a coin with King Adolf on it?"

"You fool! Nobody in Paris would be carrying a coin from the King of Germany, not unless he had done some business with his representatives, or was working for the man himself!"

De Rohan Residence
Paris, Kingdom of France

Marcus had avoided any mention of his encounter with Lord Victor when he had updated Lord Charles on their progress yesterday, but with Victor's death, there was no longer any danger to the man, and should they be overheard, or the conversation shared, no more harm could be done.

It was unfortunate, though it did give him the opportunity to ask questions freely that might yield additional information.

"I was in the third row, so luckily only twisted my knee. Many were less fortunate, with many a bone fractured that day. Those responsible were flogged. They should have been hanged for their incompetence, but I suppose forgiveness is the Christian way."

Marcus nodded, motioning at Charles' legs. "And now?"

He gingerly raised his right leg slightly, bending it at the knee. "I find I favor it from time to time, but it's almost completely healed."

"Did you require a cane?"

"I should say so! For the first week I could barely get out of bed, the second I could barely put any pressure on it whatsoever." He grunted. "I think cane sales went up in the city that first week. Half the Court required them, ladies as well." He shook his head. "They should have been drawn and quartered," he muttered. He raised his voice, jabbing at the air between them. "You know, this is what happens when you give the contract to the lowest bidder. Nobody thought to check if they were competent!" He growled. "And the embarrassment to the King! Do you realize how many foreign dignitaries were there? Many of them were injured as well! What message do you think they sent back to their lieges of French competence? A debacle if there ever was one!"

Marcus took the opportunity to pick up on something Charles said. "Speaking of foreign intrigue, what is your opinion of the truce between France and Flanders?"

Charles halted his rant, his eyebrows rising. "What has that to do with anything?"

Marcus shrugged. "Perhaps nothing, perhaps a great deal."

Charles paused, regarding Marcus before answering. "Well, I support it, of course. Anything to avoid war."

"Are there those in the Court who oppose it?"

Charles frowned. "Sadly, yes, there are some. Too many, in fact, though they have been silenced for the most part now that the truce has been signed and the King has indicated his full support."

"How split would you say the Court was?"

Charles sat behind his desk, wincing slightly. "Fairly evenly, I'm disappointed to say." He paused. "Say, that *is* something, isn't it?" He smiled, wagging a finger at Marcus. "You, my good sir, are far more clever than I have given you credit for. You're suggesting that whoever is behind these accusations is trying to tip the balance of those who would advise the King, in favor of war?"

Marcus shrugged again, but remained silent, letting the man run with his thoughts.

"Yes, yes, that is an interesting idea. Those accused are all wives of men who supported the truce, including me. Should we lose status, those who supported our position because of our influence, may be convinced to change their opinion." He batted his hand at the idea. "Preposterous. Who would go to so much trouble to provoke a war? I cannot believe a Frenchman could be behind this, and Flanders was handily defeated in our first encounters—there's simply no way they could want war." He shook his head. "This must just be a coincidence."

Marcus nodded slowly. "Perhaps you are right." He retrieved the list of names Victor had died obtaining. "I was wondering if you could look at this list for me, and indicate who you remember might have been injured." He handed the list to Charles, whose eyebrows climbed as he scanned it.

"Where did you get this?"

"From Lord Victor."

Charles paused, shaking his head. "A tragedy what happened to him. To think we aren't even safe on Palace grounds now. Something has to be done about crime in this city."

"So, you think it was random?"

Charles glanced up from the list. "Wasn't it? Somebody must have sneaked over the walls and accosted him. His purse was found missing, as was a ring his wife swore he never removed."

Marcus nodded in agreement, though he didn't share the theory. "Perhaps."

Charles returned his attention to the list, running his finger down the names, pausing on many of them. He sighed. "I'm afraid so many were injured, I can't say for certain if I would remember with any level of accuracy." He looked up. "Why is this important?"

"From our questioning, we have determined that a man who required a cane several months ago, but no longer does, may be involved."

Charles rolled his eyes. "If that's your only lead, I'll surrender to you now." He chuckled as he grabbed a quill, dipping it in ink before running down the list again, checking off several names. "Wait, you're sure it's a man?"

"Yes."

"Very well, I'll leave off the women, then. And they must have used a cane?"

Marcus nodded. "Yes."

Charles shook his head. "No. They may not have wanted to use one in the Court, lest they be perceived as weak. I'll include any I thought *might* have had trouble walking but were attempting to hide it." At least several dozen names were checked off.

Marcus pointed at the abridged list. "Are any of these men foreign, by chance, or have any dealings with foreign governments?"

Charles grunted. "So, we're back to your theory that someone, perhaps a foreign power, is trying to trigger a war between France and Flanders?"

"Lord Victor's theory, a theory for which he died."

"Assuming it wasn't a random attack." Charles waved his hand, dismissing any response, instead reviewing the list again, jotting down several notes. He

161

handed the pages back to Marcus. "Hopefully this will assist you."

Marcus bowed. "Hopefully, though as you say, it is probably just coincidence." He stuffed the pages under his chainmail. "Has there been any word from your staff on who might have given the chambermaid the note you received?"

Charles leaned back and shook his head. "None. As you may have noticed upon your arrival, security is now much tighter than it was just this morning, and certainly tighter than when the note arrived." He drew a deep breath then exhaled loudly. "I fear someone must have gained entry under false pretenses, and delivered the message to my wife's chambermaid."

"It's the likeliest explanation," agreed Marcus. "May I have it?"

Charles' eyebrows climbed his forehead. "For what purpose?"

"It's a piece of evidence and should be protected, in case you have a traitor in your midst."

Charles considered his explanation, his head slowly bobbing, then opened a drawer in his desk, retrieving a folded piece of paper. "Here you go. And when this matter is over, destroy it. I don't want any reminder of the affair." He sighed, staring up at Marcus. "And I suppose you still will not tell me where my wife is?"

"She is safe, Milord, I assure you."

"How can you be certain?"

"We were followed last night, and the threat was eliminated."

Charles leaned forward, concern on his face. "Really? And what of next time? What if you don't spot your pursuers?"

Marcus shook his head. "There won't be a next time. I have no intention of seeing your wife until this matter is settled. And as no one knows where she is beyond my sergeant and I, there is no risk of her being discovered. Rest assured, Milord, she is secure, and will be returned to you as soon as it is safe to do so."

Charles frowned. "I see I have no choice but to trust in you, though I will say the captain of my guard seems to think you are her greatest threat."

Marcus allowed himself a slight smile, far slighter than Simon's grin. "And did I have the pleasure of his company at my home the other day?"

"Yes, you did."

Marcus bowed slightly. "I am pleased to hear he's still alive. And the others? I trust they are recovering?"

Charles smiled slightly. "Yes."

"That is indeed good news. As I'm sure you're aware, we maimed, rather than killed, as we weren't clear on the situation. Now that we are, I can assure you, should anyone attempt to take your wife, they will be shown no quarter."

Charles grunted. "Of course, I would expect no less."

Marcus motioned toward the door. "Now, sir, if you'll excuse us, we have a busy day."

Charles rose. "Where does your investigation lead you now?"

"Back to Sir Denys'."

Charles frowned at the mention of the man's name. "Why? Is he now a suspect?"

Marcus shook his head, tapping where he had placed the papers. "No, but his name is on the list, and perhaps his recollection of things will fill in some of the blanks you warned may be in your memory."

Charles nodded. "You know, he opposed the treaty."

Marcus regarded him. "Did he, now?"

Charles shrugged. "Perhaps merely a coincidence."

"Perhaps."

"But if it isn't, and this scandal is indeed designed to break the truce, he would be someone who might be behind it."

Marcus bowed. "Thank you for your counsel. We will be careful what we say in his presence."

Durant Residence
Paris, Kingdom of France

Simone Thibault tiptoed toward the rear entrance of her decrepit accommodations, noting with a snort that the two men supposedly guarding them were asleep at their posts.

Though the annoying dog wasn't.

It growled at her, waking Jeremy.

Perhaps that's why he felt he could sleep.

He groaned as he stretched, then finally took notice of her as her hand reached the door. "Where are you going?"

"To take care of my business."

His eyes narrowed. "Excuse me?"

"To drop my knickers and rid myself of last night's feast!"

Jeremy blushed. "Oh, umm, I'm sorry."

"Go back to sleep, I'll be a while."

He grinned. "I've been there, but I should get up."

"Nonsense. You were up all night keeping us safe. Let us keep watch during the day."

Jeremy nodded, getting comfortable again, his eyes already drooping. She stepped outside, the outhouse to the left, attached to the rear of the building. She opened the door and stepped inside, making quick work of it, then left as quietly as she could, closing the door gently. She rushed down the alleyway and into the main street that passed in front of Thomas' home, spotting a boy of a questionable sort.

"Lad, come here."

The boy approached with the wariness of one with experience on the streets. "What do you want?"

"I have a job for you, if you're interested."

The boy eyed him with suspicion. "If there's money in it, I am."

"There is." She dropped a coin into his palm and his eyes shot wide. "I need you to go to the Swan tavern. Do you know where it is?"

The boy's head bobbed vigorously, his eyes still glued to the coin. "I used to live near there before my grandmother died."

"Excellent. Go to the bartender, and tell him Mrs. Thibault sent you, and that I need Enzo to come back with you." She pointed at the ground floor of Thomas' building. "I need you to bring him to that old shop, understood?"

The boy nodded. "Tell the bartender at the Swan that Mrs. Thibault needs Mr. Enzo to come back with me."

"Perfect! And when you return, there will be two more of those," she said, pointing at his clenched fist containing his down payment.

His eyes shot wide. "Yes, ma'am!" He sprinted in the opposite direction, and she hurried back to her uncomfortable prison before someone checked on her, a smile spreading.

As soon as Enzo arrives, things will change.

En Route to the de Montfort Residence
Paris, Kingdom of France

"I noticed you didn't mention the German coins we found."

Marcus glanced over at Simon, riding beside him on his borrowed horse. "No, I think we should keep that to ourselves. He might repeat our suspicions to someone else, and word could spread. We don't want whoever is behind this to disappear before we can have them arrested."

Simon nodded, a frown spreading. "And what if the King is behind this?"

Marcus sighed, the thought having occurred to him as well. He didn't trust the man at all, not after his experiences of a few weeks ago, and not with his open hostility toward the Order Marcus had dedicated his life to. "Then I fear there is little we can do, though in this case, I still think that he isn't. If he wanted to end the truce, he would simply do it."

Simon grunted. "True. Do you think Denys could be the one?"

Marcus chuckled. "Well, Lord Charles certainly seemed eager to let us know he was opposed to the truce, though if he were, how does carrying on an affair with someone help him? He too is committing a crime in so doing, not just Lady Joanne."

"Do you think they have arrested him?"

Marcus urged his horse forward a little quicker with the suggestion. "The men with whom the wives were accused of having the affairs weren't named when the charges were read in the Court, which I found odd. It was as if they were only concerned with one side of the crime."

"To discredit their husbands?"

"That's my thinking. If a man can't control his wife, he can't be relied upon in matters of true importance." He stared at Sir Denys' estate as they rounded a bend in the road. "Can you ever imagine living in such a place?"

Simon laughed. "I wouldn't know what to do with myself. I think I'd be ashamed. To have so much, when so many have so little?"

Marcus agreed. "I wonder if these men have any idea how easy their lives are compared to the masses that surround them."

Simon tossed his head back, laughing even harder. "They probably think they're doing good by the poor, in having such large staffs."

Marcus smiled. "True, and I guess in a way they are. Gainful employment in a safe environment is charitable in a way, I suppose, but seeing this"—he waved his hand at the large estate—"makes me thankful I took a vow of poverty when joining the Templars. Because of it, I'll never have to face such choices."

"Or worry about your wife committing adultery."

Marcus laughed. "Nor that!"

They approached the open gate and the guard waved them through, their Templar surcoats all that was needed. They approached the large home and dismounted, their horses taken by a stable boy.

"When will you be needing them back, sir?"

"In short order. We won't be here very long."

"Very well, sir, I'll tend to them quickly."

"Thank you, son."

Sir Denys appeared on the steps, waving at them, a broad smile greeting them. "Ahh, Sir Marcus, so good to see you. Do you have news?"

Marcus bowed. "Little, though I do have questions, if you have the time."

Denys motioned toward the entrance. "I do, though even if I didn't, one must make the time for events such as these. How may I help you?"

Marcus and Simon followed him inside. "I have a list I would like you to look at for me." He pulled out the pages, handing them to Denys. "It is a list of guests at the jousting tournament, on August ninth."

Denys shook his head, glancing through the pages as he led them to his office. "Now that was a day! I nearly broke my neck!" He pointed at some of Charles' notes. "What are these?"

"Notes from Lord Charles. I'd like you to go through the list and indicate any of the men you remember being injured, who might have required a cane, and if they had any associations with foreign governments."

Denys took a seat behind his desk, grabbing a quill and dipping it in ink. "Why? What does that have to do with anything?"

"We think the man involved required a cane after the accident, but no longer does."

"Huh. Give me a moment." He quickly scanned the list, adding only two checks, and no notes. "It looks like Lord Charles' was very thorough. I agree with everything he indicated, and I think he only

169

missed a few, though I too could have missed some. It was a tragedy of immense proportions, I tell you. So many injured, and so many badly. I was lucky to escape with my life, what with being relegated to the back row with the highest possible drop. As soon as I felt it begin to collapse, I leaped to the ground and was able to roll out of the way. I still landed on my hip, bruising it horribly. I don't think I walked properly for weeks." He handed the pages back. "Was that all you required?"

Marcus stuffed the pages out of sight, and retrieved the letter he had procured from Charles. "One more thing, if you would. Can you please read this, and tell me if you notice anything?" He handed Denys the letter, the man's nostrils flaring as he read the contents. "So, this is what would have me condemned." He sighed, shaking his head. "Nothing seems unusual, though you will have noticed the writer is left-handed."

Marcus leaned forward, examining the letter. "Why, I suppose he is. Perhaps, though, he is trying to make us *think* he is."

Denys shook his head, pointing at the writing. "This is a practiced hand. It is difficult to fake writing with the other hand. I myself am left-handed, but my parents were fastidious about making sure I was cured of that ailment. Now, after much practice, I can write equally well with both hands."

Simon grunted. "Then perhaps you wrote this."

Denys laughed, holding out his arms, his wrists pressed together as if awaiting irons. "Yes, arrest me now! I revealed myself to the husband of my lover, who in fact wasn't her husband at all!" Gloom replaced the laughter. "I'm sorry, but I still can't believe what is happening. I just received word that the women have all confessed to their affairs, which means their situations are different than mine, since we all now agree that Lady Joanne is innocent, despite being named in the same breath as the others. Why should she alone be innocent, while none of the others were?"

"Perhaps they were tortured into false confessions," suggested Marcus.

Denys paled slightly. "Unfortunately, a contact of mine has confirmed they were tortured. Thank God you were able to hide Lady Joanne, otherwise she too would have been."

Marcus nodded. "Do we know yet who their partners were in their adultery?"

Denys leaped from his chair, tossing the letter back on his desk. "Yes, as a matter of fact!" He shook his head, pacing back and forth behind his desk. "And this is the most troubling thing! This morning, three young men, quite dashing and eloquent, if what I have been told is correct, presented themselves to the Court, claiming they had been paid by the husbands to seduce their wives, in the hopes they may produce male heirs! Can you believe such a thing!"

Marcus had to admit he didn't. It was a fantastic idea, though under French law, if a man died without a male heir, the consequences could be horrific for what remained of his family. "I must admit, Sir Denys, that this comes as quite the shock."

Denys' head bobbed vigorously. "To me as well! It hadn't occurred to me until I heard it, that these three men had no male heirs, only daughters, or no children at all! According to the message I received, their husbands had discussed it among themselves, after a friend had died at the stage collapse, leaving no male heir. His wife and daughters now have had to rely upon the charity of others since, much of their estate seized to pay debts, and with her husband's title lost, so were his taxable estates. These men decided they didn't want their wives to face such a fate, so embarked upon this unholy exercise in the hopes of avoiding any future horrors."

Denys dropped back into his chair, and Marcus took up the pacing in front of the desk, his jaw clenched, absorbing everything said. Could they have been wrong about everything? Was there no conspiracy involving the German King to force France and Flanders into war, but instead, this was all an exercise in dealing with the lack of male heirs to inherit the titles of their fathers?

Though why just these three men? And why were they all in favor of the treaty? Was that just a coincidence?

No, perhaps not. It would make sense that like-minded men would associate, and would be friends. They could discuss their shared problems, and the tragedy of the stage collapse could indeed have triggered such discussions. Yet to take it to the extreme of soliciting young men to bed their wives?

He knew nothing of women, of marriage, or of love. Perhaps these things were possible, though he thought it preposterous. He looked at Denys. "Do you believe their story?"

Denys shrugged. "I can see no reason for them to lie. These men are going to die horrible deaths should the King order it. They have committed a crime, and a sin. In fact, the husbands too could be punished. I think it is safe to say that their days as members of the Court are numbered. The very notion that one would engage in such an undertaking boggles the mind."

"I'm glad to see I'm not the only one shocked about this." Marcus paused. "Does Lord Charles have a son?"

Denys thought for a moment. "Not that I'm aware of, but if they wanted to implicate him in the same affair, why wouldn't they just have a fourth man confess? Why employ an imposter and involve me?" He shook his head. "It makes no sense."

Marcus frowned. "I agree, it does make no sense, unless they are lying, which again, has dire consequences for them."

Denys shifted in his chair. "I can't see why they would. They face certain death. And even if they are, why drag Lord Charles into it?" He paused, raising a finger. "Wait. We're forgetting that I met my Lady Joanne two months ago, and the stage collapse was only three months ago. Is it even possible for someone to have caught wind of this plan, and moved that quickly to try and implicate Lord Charles? The timing doesn't seem to make sense to me."

Simon cleared his throat. "That's true, sir. And Mrs. Thibault said that she had been hired to train Miss Girard *three* months ago. They can't be related. There's just not enough time."

Marcus agreed with his sergeant's assessment. "Yes, though perhaps someone caught wind of what these men were up to, and decided to take advantage of it after the fact." He looked at Denys. "Have the husbands responded yet to these accusations?"

"Not that I'm aware of, however, I suspect they'll be arrested soon."

"Do you know them well enough that they might take a meeting with you?"

Denys tapped his chin for a moment. "On any other day, I would say yes, but today? With all that is happening? I'd be surprised." He eyed Marcus, a smile spreading. "But with you at my side, I hardly think any would say no."

Marcus headed for the door. "Then with all due haste, we must meet with at least one of these men before they are arrested, and perhaps silenced permanently."

Durant Residence
Paris, Kingdom of France

Someone knocked on the door, silencing those gathered in Thomas Durant's father's storefront. David rose, drawing his sword, as Jeremy did the same, taking a hold of Tanya's collar as she growled.

"Who could that be?" asked David of no one in particular.

"Is that you, Enzo?" called Simone Thibault, struggling to her feet.

"Yes, ma'am."

"Let him in, let him in!"

David glared at her. "Who the hell is that?"

"One of my men. He's harmless. Let him in before he raises a fuss and draws attention."

Rage raced through David, but he had no choice, Enzo, whoever he was, pounding on the door again. He opened it, his eyes bulging at the massive wall of muscle filling the doorway.

"Get inside, get inside!" urged Thibault, clearly pleased to see the man. He crouched, entering, as David quickly closed the door, peering out through the cracks in one of the boarded-up windows. "How did you find us?"

"I got the mistress' message."

David's jaw dropped as the room erupted in anger, all of it aimed at Thibault. "What is he talking about?"

Thibault seemed unconcerned with the vitriol aimed her way. "I sent for him this morning."

"When?"

"When I went to the bathroom."

David stared at a horrified Jeremy. "I-I'm sorry, she tricked me!"

But there was no time for blame. David stared at Enzo. "Were you followed?"

"Of course not."

David peered out the window, examining the crowds passing, and spotted a man across the street, lurking in the shadows, staring at their hideout. "You were." He cursed, throwing up his hands. "Now what are we going to do?"

Jeremy rushed forward, looking out the window himself. "If it's only him, then he won't report back until he's confirmed she's here."

David agreed. "Right, but how long will he wait? Eventually, he's going to report back and at least relay his suspicions." He jabbed a finger at Thibault. "Thanks to you, we're no longer safe here, and we have nowhere to go! Why would you do such a thing? Why would you send for him?"

Thibault shrugged. "I'm sick and tired of living like a prisoner and a peasant. I wanted him to fetch some of my things."

Lady Joanne gasped. "Of all the selfish things! I'm not used to living like this either, but do you see me complaining? One must make do under such circumstances! Sir Marcus and Simon are out there risking their lives for us, and they trusted all of us to do nothing that could put us at risk!"

David took another look, the man still across the street, still staring at the shop. "He's still there, and he's definitely watching the place." He frowned. "We have no choice but to try and eliminate him, but if he gets away, or has an accomplice, or has already sent word back to his master, our time here is finished."

Joanne rose. "I don't think we have a choice. We have to go to my husband, and pray he'll take us in. He knows I'm innocent. I can't see him saying no."

Jeremy frowned. "Sir Marcus didn't want us to do that, but I don't see that we have a choice either. At least there, we should be able to get word to Sir Marcus for instructions."

David's chest was tight, not used to having such decisions thrust upon him, but he had been left in charge, and now he had to manage the situation. He looked around the room, shaking his head. "There are six of us, and we have three horses. We'll have to double-up."

"That'll make for a sight," muttered Jeremy.

Thomas shook his head. "Not in these parts, but you're right, once we enter your part of the city, Milady, we will stand out."

Jeremy started gathering their things. "At that point, we can dismount and walk the horses with the ladies."

David shook his head. "Then it would be open season on us. We must make all haste." He pointed at Thibault. "This is your doing. Give Master Thomas some money so he can hire us three more horses."

She glared at him for a moment before finally acquiescing, fishing several coins from her purse and handing them to Thomas.

"Make it quick!" said David, and Thomas bolted toward the front door. David caught him before he could open it. "Go out the back, and bring them there. We don't want whoever's watching to see anything in the front."

Thomas nodded. "Y-yes." He headed out the back, the door slamming shut a moment later.

Thibault sat in one of the two chairs. "There, problem solved. We'll have six horses, and we can move swiftly to safety."

David shook his head. "We'll be followed, and perhaps intercepted."

She batted her hand at his statement. "We'll ride hard and fast."

David laughed. "Forgive me, but other than myself and David, none of you are experienced enough on a horse to ride in such a way."

"You'd be surprised."

"Yes, I would be. We've been riding for over a decade in battle, you haven't. Racing a horse through the streets of a city, with people in the way, is no easy task, especially when one's attention is divided by the road ahead, and possible pursuers behind."

Jeremy stared out the window. "We need to deal with our problem first, and before Thomas returns."

David looked at him. "What do you propose?"

Jeremy sighed. "I can think of only one thing, but if we're wrong, and this is just some innocent man waiting for someone, it would be murder."

Joanne stepped forward, wringing her hands. "Is there any way we can be sure?"

David shrugged. "Challenge him?"

Jeremy eyed him. "What do you mean?"

David pointed at his bow on the table. "You get on the roof, and I'll go outside and ask what his business is. If he has a reasonable answer, I'll return. If he doesn't, I'll signal you."

Jeremy pursed his lips then nodded. "Sounds like a plan to me."

"Then let's make haste, there isn't a moment to lose."

En Route to Lord Gaspard de Laval's Residence
Paris, Kingdom of France

Marcus, Simon, and Sir Denys rode swiftly to the home of the nearest husband now accused of involvement in the troubling plot of ensuring a male heir. The very notion disgusted Marcus, and he still couldn't believe what he had been told. Denys had shown him the letter as they waited for his horse to be fetched, confirming all the sordid details.

It was stunning.

Yet still didn't explain why Lord Charles and his wife Joanne, along with her purported lover, Sir Denys, were involved.

There were three men who had come forward, not four, and the wives had confessed to the affairs, apparently under torture.

He was convinced something else was going on, perhaps having attached itself to another scandal out of convenience.

Denys pointed ahead. "This is it!"

They slowed as they approached the gate, and after a few moments, were allowed entry and led to Lord Gaspard's office. They were announced, then barely acknowledged by the man who appeared to be in a near panic as he searched his desk for something.

Denys stepped forward. "Lord Gaspard, I'm sorry to disturb you at this desperate time, however these men have questions for you that could help them resolve this situation in your favor."

This brought Gaspard to a halt, and he finally looked up at them, his eyes coming to rest on the bright red of the cross emblazoned on Marcus' surcoat. "A Templar Knight." He shook his head. "You're the only reason I agreed to see you. Make it quick, they'll be here any moment." He dropped back into his chair, his shoulders slumping in defeat. "Have you heard what these heathens have accused me of?"

Marcus stepped forward. "Then it isn't true?"

"Of course it isn't!" Gaspard stared at him. "What business is this of the Templars?"

Marcus bowed. "I am Sir Marcus de Rancourt, cousin of the Lady Joanne de Rohan. She has asked me to act on her behalf in these matters."

Gaspard nodded slowly. "That's right, she's mixed up in this thing too." He bolted forward in his chair, jabbing a finger at his desk. "This entire thing is nonsense! I have a male heir!"

Denys' eyebrows shot up. "You do? I thought you had no children."

"I don't, but I have a younger brother. He'll inherit if I die, and we are on excellent terms. There's no risk to my wife of losing her standing. He will inherit my title, and he has three sons of his own to continue the family line and care for my wife and daughters. This entire thing is preposterous!"

Marcus processed this new information. Surely if someone were indeed manipulating this affair, they would have known this fact. "Was this publicly known?"

Gaspard shrugged. "I don't know. He lives up north, and we rarely see each other, though we correspond regularly. It's not a secret, though not really discussed, so perhaps not."

"And what of the others? Do they have heirs?"

Gaspard paused. "Well, Lord Olivier, I'm not sure. I know both he and Lord Jean have no sons, but I think Lord Jean has a brother, though I can't be certain." He threw up his hands. "These things aren't exactly a topic of conversation. When we converse, it is of the affairs of state, not who would inherit our estates should we meet an untimely demise!"

Marcus nodded. "What will you do?"

Gaspard grabbed at the back of his neck with his hand, squeezing. "Throw myself on the mercy of the Court, I suppose. I can think of nothing else."

Simon cleared his throat. "Wouldn't telling them what you just told us clear your good name?"

Gaspard exploded, his cheeks burning red. "You daft fool! Don't you realize what is going on here? We're being set up by someone! They've manufactured evidence against us to destroy us. Just this morning I received word that my wife has already signed a confession, admitting to the affair, and that it was sanctioned by me in the hopes of having a son, so it would be *my* lineage that would continue the family name, and not my brother's! They've thought of everything!"

Marcus frowned at this revelation. It would appear that those involved *did* know Gaspard had a male heir, and were using the excuse of lineage instead. Yet none of this explained Lady Joanne's involvement.

Denys rubbed his chin. "Yes, but who are *they*?"

"If I knew, do you not think I'd tell you?"

Marcus returned to Lord Victor's theory. "What about the truce?"

Gaspard eyed him. "What truce?"

"Between France and Flanders. Could this have something to do with that?"

Gaspard paused, his mouth slowly opening as if this possibility had never occurred to him. "What would make you say that?"

"It's been pointed out to me that those involved are all in favor of the treaty. Embarrassing you would perhaps sway the Court to change its opinion in favor of war."

Gaspard's eyes widened. "But that would be insane! Who would possibly want war? The King certainly doesn't seem to."

Marcus pressed on. "But the Court was split, was it not?"

"Well, yes, many did want war, but myself and—" His eyes widened further. "And Lords Olivier and Jean, as well as Lord Charles, argued hard against rejecting the truce. We felt, in the end, it was in France's best interest to agree to peace, rather than go to the expense of yet another war with little benefit, especially with the English involved." He paled. "But with us out of the way, those who oppose peace could prevail, and sway the King to their way of thinking." He shook his head. "But I can't believe anyone could truly want such a thing."

Marcus decided to reveal the one thing he had been holding back. "What of King Adolf of Germany?"

Gaspard's eyes narrowed. "Why would you—?"

"Sir, they're here!" shouted someone down the hall, heavy footfalls getting nearer. The door opened and one of the servants entered, gasping for breath. "Sir, they're here!"

Marcus turned. "Who?"

"The King's Personal Guard. They say they have a warrant for the master's arrest."

Gaspard rose, rounding his desk, then grabbed Marcus by the arm. "You believe I'm innocent?"

Marcus nodded. "I do."

"Then you must do whatever you can to prove it, otherwise it could mean war."

Durant Residence
Paris, Kingdom of France

David took a deep breath as he peered through the boards at the man watching them. Jeremy should be on the roof by now, though he couldn't risk going early. He had to wait for confirmation. Footsteps approaching from behind him delivered it.

"He's in position," hissed Lady Joanne, who had climbed the back stairs with Jeremy, waiting for his signal.

"Good." He turned and handed Tanya's leash to her. "Keep a good grip on her, but if you have to, let her go. She probably outweighs you, and will just drag you if she's so inclined."

"I understand."

"And if anything goes wrong, go out the back, get on our horses, and head to the Templar headquarters. You remember how to get there?"

She nodded. "Yes." She placed a hand on his arm. "But nothing will go wrong. You'll be all right."

He smiled at her. "I hope so. But be ready, understood?"

"Yes." She gave him a quick hug and he blushed, his heart racing at what was his first since childhood.

It felt good.

He let go of the leash and pointed at Tanya. "You be good, or Sir Marcus will be cross with you, understood?"

The dog barked, her tail wagging.

185

"All right, let's do this." David opened the door and stepped outside, closing it behind him. He strode toward the man across the street with purpose, though not at a run—even an innocent man would balk at that. He waved pleasantly. "Excuse me, sir, but can I ask what your business is here?"

The man's eyes bulged, and he opened his mouth, saying nothing, instead making a string of indecisive sounds as if searching for the words.

"I only ask because you've been staring at my friend's home for some time now, and you're making him nervous."

The man's eyes darted from left to right, then he reached for his sword as a roar erupted from within.

I guess that's an answer.

David spun and raced back toward Thomas' home, not bothering with a subtle signal for Jeremy as the man chased after him, his sword gripped in both hands over his head.

The crisp sound of a well-loosed arrow whipped past him from overhead, the distinct thud followed by a gasped cry signaling success. He eased up then came to a stop, his pursuer now prone in the mud, his chest heaving out its last breaths as a large pool of blood spread, an artery obviously hit.

A horse whinnied to his right and David spun to see another man racing away. David looked about and spotted a horse tied up across the street. He raced over and untied it, then swung into the saddle. "Jeremy!" He held up his hand as he urged the horse back toward Thomas'. Jeremy tossed down his bow and David easily caught it then the quiver filled with arrows. He sent his horse into a gallop after the man, still visible in the distance, as he slung the quiver over his shoulder, using his knees to control the steed until he got settled.

He leaned forward, smacking the side of the unfamiliar horse, urging her onward as he closed the gap with the rider ahead of him, his adversary forced to deal with the crowds that filled the street, David taking advantage of the already parted souls. As he neared, he reached behind him and drew an arrow, continuing the chase. His heart slammed with excitement, an excitement he desperately missed, and as he neared, he could picture the enemy ahead in Saracen garb, the desert sand whipping about him, the dry air parching his mouth.

Oh, Lord, how I wish I still served thee!

Yet wasn't he? He was protecting an innocent woman, and one not so innocent, from harm. He was helping his master care for three children back at the farm. Was this not the Lord's work?

It was.

It just wasn't as exciting, and that was selfish. Excitement was to satisfy the weaknesses of man, not the glory of God.

And didn't his heart yet beat with the thrill of the chase at this very moment? Life in the Holy Land was filled with battles, but they weren't every day. Most of it was spent in prayer or drills. And during patrols, it was a life of being constantly on edge, of always wondering what lurked in the shadows, of what might attack you next.

Here, in France, on the farm, he felt at peace for the first time in over a decade, and he was enjoying it. He was sure that as time went on, and they planted then harvested crops, he would reap the satisfaction of hard work paying off, and if the past few weeks were any indication, he might still get the adventure he craved.

After all, they were still Templars, and couldn't simply sit back and watch injustice go unpunished around them.

Now you're mine.

He was finally close enough to make the kill without harming those still in the streets. The man glanced over his shoulder at him, and David kept leaning forward, not revealing the bow at his side. The man faced forward again, unsuspecting, and David swiftly took aim and shot, the arrow sailing through the air, perfectly loosed.

It impacted his opponent square in the back. He threw his arms out in agony as his neck bent backward. A cry erupted before he slumped forward in his saddle, his horse slowing. David quickly reached him, taking the horse by the lead, bringing it to a stop. He grabbed the man by the chin, a weak moan escaping before David noticed with satisfaction that the arrow had pierced the man's chest, the tip visible through what was merely a tunic.

No armor?

The other man hadn't worn any either. These men were clearly meant to blend in, and armor would have prevented that.

The decision had doomed them.

He turned his horse back toward Thomas' as a crowd gathered, fear growing in him at the thought there might have been a third man.

Thomas led the three horses down the alleyway behind his home. There had been a lot of surprised looks when he had handed over the coins to pay for the beasts, those in the neighborhood knowing that he was destitute. But when he had explained they weren't for him, the questions had been satisfied, and the despair he was consumed by was renewed.

Of course they weren't for him.

What would he, a starving peasant, need with three horses? And where would he get such money?

It had felt good, though, if for only a moment. Money in his palm was something he wasn't used to, and should he live out his life working a farm with Sir Marcus, he would probably never feel it again.

But with Mrs. Thibault? He might feel it all the time. His heart fluttered with the thought. Enough money never to go wanting again. Though could he live with himself? She was clearly an unsavory sort—a criminal. What crimes would she involve him in should he fall under her employ?

He couldn't imagine anything too sordid. After all, she wanted him for his brains, not his brawn. He looked down at his emaciated frame.

Definitely not his brawn.

And how much trouble could he get in, merely reading and writing?

His father had been a forger. A criminal. And he had never done anything as untoward as killing or maiming. He had probably never even met any of his victims, as they weren't his. They were the victims of those who hired him. He merely provided a service. If others got hurt, it wasn't his father's fault, it was that of the man who had hired him.

As it would be with Mrs. Thibault. If he were merely reading and writing for her, and she then used his skills to hurt others, he wasn't responsible, she was. He was only a tool. Did one blame the sword that killed the man, or the person who wielded it? What about the sword's maker?

The answer was obvious.

Yet for some reason, he still felt guilty even contemplating working for her, especially with Sir Marcus' offer there for the taking. An honest life of hard labor. And as the man had said, he could just go to the farm for a while until back on his feet. It would give him time to think, to figure out what he wanted to do with his life. There was still the possibility of joining the Templars. He couldn't be a knight, of course, as he had no royal lineage, but the Order was in need of skilled people to help administer their vast holdings, and with his ability to read and write, he would probably be welcomed into the fold.

Though it would be a poor life. Yes, it would be rewarding in that he would be serving God and something bigger than himself, but it would be merely the existence of an employed peasant.

He wanted more.

He sighed as his dilapidated home came into sight.

Then frowned at the flurry of activity behind it as the three horses already there were quickly prepared.

He urged his three forward, coming to a halt to see Jeremy and Enzo at work. "What's happened?"

"He was watching the place as we suspected." Jeremy tightened the saddle. "I took him down, but there was another. David took after him and isn't back yet. We need to be ready to go at once." He glanced at the three new horses. "Double-check them. We will be riding hard and fast, and can't risk anyone falling off from a loose saddle."

Thomas nodded, climbing off his horse and getting to work, when pounding hoofs approached from the opposite direction. Jeremy stepped into the alley, drawing his sword, before sheathing it with a sigh of relief.

"David! I feared the worst!"

David brought his horse to a halt. "As did I, but I got him. We must leave now, there's no time to lose. I fear there may be others."

"Why?"

"If there were two, then why both wait? Wouldn't one go and tell the others where they were, so reinforcements could be fetched?"

Jeremy regarded him. "What are you saying?"

"I'm saying they *did* send someone, so there was at least a third. Others could be arriving at any moment, and we can't be here." He pointed at the door. "Get the others. I'm going to return this horse. I'll be back in a moment." He turned his horse around and rushed back down the alley, out of sight a moment later.

Thomas finished checking his three horses as Jeremy disappeared inside. The two ladies, along with the dog Tanya, appeared shortly after, and Thomas helped Lady Joanne onto one of the new horses as Enzo helped his mistress onto another. Thomas, Jeremy, and Enzo mounted as David tore around the corner at a sprint, leaping onto the back of the lone remaining horse.

"Let's go!" They moved forward, and David turned in his saddle, looking at Joanne. "Milady, you will have to guide us, so stay just behind me."

"Very well."

They turned out of the alleyway, making for the main street that ran in front of Thomas' home, then turned left. Six horses and an excited dog made for quite the entourage, and the noise of the hooves served as an alarm to those in their path, the crowds parting for them, allowing them to keep a good pace the entire way. It felt like hours, his heart hammering the entire time, his hands gripping the reins tighter than they should, as every rider was suspect, every angry eye a threat—but it was half an hour at best.

The city might have been big, but it was nothing compared to the vast lands that surrounded it, lands Thomas could say he had barely seen. They quickly left his neighborhood far behind, and after crossing a bridge, he found his mouth agape at the estates that lined the road, memories returning of his youth when he visited here from time to time to see his forbidden childhood friend.

His chest tightened at the memories.

At the betrayal.

"Behind us!"

Thomas snapped out of his reverie, turning to see Jeremy falling back, David slowing to join him, pointing at Lady Joanne.

"Keep going!"

"We're almost there!" she replied, urging her horse back to a full gallop. Thomas hesitated to join her and the others, his horse continuing to slow, when David made the decision for him.

"Go, Master Thomas! Defend them if needed!"

Thomas drew in a deep breath, nodding, then urged his steed after the others, a few moments passing before he realized he had no sword in which to defend anyone.

He said it to save your life.

He turned back to see David and Jeremy, high in their saddles, arrows loosed in rapid succession at a group of riders charging toward them. One after the other they fell, yet they kept coming, and Thomas lost sight of them as he rounded a bend in the road. His chest ached at how useless he felt, how if only he were trained, he might have been able to remain behind and help those brave men.

But he was nothing.

Not even a dreamer.

He had to do better. He had to make a better life for himself.

"Open the gates!" cried Lady Joanne ahead of them, and he looked up to see the gates of a large estate swing open, Joanne surging through to safety followed by the others. He cleared the walls and the gates began to swing shut when he stopped his horse and leaped off, rushing back.

"Wait! There are still two more!" He ran back onto the road, peering into the distance, his pulse pounding from the ride and the fear, then breathed a sigh of relief as Jeremy rounded the bend, galloping hard, David a short distance behind him. He waved at them, urging them on, his heart nearly stopping when he saw two men in pursuit. He slowly stepped back toward the gates as they neared. "Hurry!" he cried, then turned on his heel to run back inside as David and

Jeremy blew past him, the guards closing the gates as the riders in pursuit slowed then turned.

"That was close!" laughed David as he dismounted, Joanne and the others rushing over.

"Oh, thank God you're all right!" she cried, giving him a quick hug. "You saved us!"

Jeremy cleared his throat. "Umm, I think *we* saved us."

Joanne laughed, giving him a hug as well, leaving the two squires with flushed cheeks.

"Is that my wife?" cried a voice, and Thomas spun to see a man running down the steps toward them, his arms outstretched.

"Oh, Charles!" cried Joanne, rushing forward and throwing herself into his arms, tears flowing freely.

"Are you all right, my love? Were you hurt?"

She shook her head. "No, these good men saved us all." She pressed a hand against her husband's chest. "You know about the letter?"

"Yes, yes. It was all lies. I know now that you would never betray me like that."

She collapsed in his arms. "Oh thank God it's over."

Her husband patted her on the back then gently pushed her away, staring into her eyes. "I'm afraid it is anything but over, my dear. We must find out who is behind this, for they may yet succeed in destroying us."

David stepped forward. "Milord, I'm sorry to interrupt this most joyous reunion, however, is our master here?"

Charles shook his head. "No, he is not, though I know where he was going. I'll have word sent at once that you have arrived." He motioned toward the house, wrapping an arm around his wife's shoulders. "Now let's get inside where it is safe. I don't want anything happening to you now that I have you back."

De Laval Residence
Paris, Kingdom of France

"What now?"

Marcus shook his head as Lord Gaspard was led away in irons, no dignity permitted by the King's Personal Guard, the intention clearly to humiliate. Whatever came of the charges, Gaspard's reputation would be sullied, perhaps permanently, convincing Marcus even more that this entire exercise was to remove four barriers to war from the King's Court.

And his only proof was several German coins found in the possession of men who could never tell their stories.

He turned to Simon. "I suggest we dismiss this ridiculous notion of male heirs, and return to our previous theory that someone is trying to end the truce with Flanders."

Sir Denys turned his back to the humiliation, clearly flustered by what he had just witnessed, the sobbing staff gathered in the courtyard not helping. "I want to know why I've been drawn into this. We still have no explanation for why someone went to all the trouble to hire and train an imposter, seduce me, then accuse Lady Joanne falsely of the same crime as these others. No imposters were involved there, as far as we know."

Marcus agreed. "No, in fact, I doubt any crime actually occurred there."

Simon's eyes narrowed. "What do you mean?"

"Think about it, this story of the husbands hiring these three men to impregnate their wives is totally reliant upon the trustworthiness of these men. We know the confessions from Lord Gaspard's wife, and any other confessions that may have been obtained, were most likely the result of threats or torture. They can easily be dismissed. It is the confessions of these three men that introduced this notion, and I for one don't believe them for a moment. And if their confessions are lies, then it is likely they've never even met the wives. I believe if we were to discover the whole truth in this matter, we would find that none of these women have ever had an affair, and that this entire web of lies is designed to discredit their husbands."

Denys sighed, his head shaking slowly. "I would agree on all three counts, yet it still doesn't explain my situation."

Marcus chewed his cheek for a moment. "Does Lord Charles have any children?"

Denys' eyes widened. "Why, yes, he does. He has a son, of age, who lives in Champagne, I believe."

Marcus' was surprised at the revelation. "I didn't think Lady Joanne was old enough to have a grown child."

"Oh, it isn't hers. Charles was married before. His wife died of some illness when the boy was about ten, I believe. Charles married Joanne shortly after. I'm afraid the boy was not pleased with the situation. He took the first opportunity to leave. From what I've heard, it broke his father's heart, but did make things at home much easier the past few years."

Marcus smiled slightly. "Then there's your answer."

Denys eyed him. "Excuse me?"

"Would you say you're close to Lord Charles?"

Denys grunted. "Not at all."

"Yet you know this story."

"The entire Court knows this—" His jaw dropped. "Oh, I see. Everyone knows the story, so everyone knows he has a male heir. They couldn't use the same story on him as they did on the others."

"Exactly. Someone is trying to draw Lord Charles into the scandal, so he too can be humiliated, though not implicated in the crime of partaking in the impregnation of his wife by another man. He'll likely be found innocent of any involvement in this scandal, but the damage will have been done." Marcus frowned. "And as to the others, I fear that things are moving so swiftly, they could be dead before we have a chance to uncover the truth."

Simon's fingers drummed the hilt of his sword. "Then what are we going to do?"

Marcus thought for a moment. There were questions that needed answering. Who had delivered the note to the chambermaid? Who had he chased that night after the murder of the imposter, Miss Girard? Who had hired the men who had followed them to Thomas Durant's? Who had killed Lord Victor? Who had hired these three men to sacrifice themselves in a false confession?

He paused, his eyebrows slowly rising. "Here's a question. Why would three men turn themselves in and confess to a horrendous crime, knowing they would face certain torture and death?"

198

Simon's head bobbed slowly. "That *is* a question, isn't it? We know they have no moral character for taking part in such a thing, so why indeed."

"Loyalty."

Marcus nodded at Denys. "Exactly. And I can think of only two reasons, and they are loyalty to one's God, or to one's master."

Simon shook his head. "No man of God would participate in such a thing."

Marcus agreed. "Which means they are loyal to their master, and I would be surprised if anyone would display such loyalty to a mere lord or duke. This is the loyalty one shows to king and country."

Denys gasped. "King Adolf? I heard you mention him earlier. Why?"

Marcus regarded Denys for a moment, then took a chance. "Two men followed us last night. We eliminated the threat, and on their persons, discovered German *groschen* coins."

Denys' eyebrows shot up. "That *is* odd. I can think of no reason why anyone in France would be carrying German currency. It isn't much evidence however, is it? We can't exactly march into the Court and accuse the King of Germany of trying to foment war between France and Flanders. And why would he? He's currently allied with England."

Marcus frowned. "I wasn't aware of that. I'm afraid my knowledge of the affairs of state is limited."

Denys' jaw slowly dropped as something occurred to him. He smiled. "Then you wouldn't know this! Several months ago, we were briefed that apparently England isn't happy with their new ally. King Adolf apparently hasn't lived up to his end of the treaty."

Marcus' head slowly bobbed. "Interesting. So perhaps he hopes to draw England into war with their ally Flanders, against France."

Denys excitedly held up a finger. "Yes! And with our problems with the Pope, and with King Adolf's family so heavily involved with the Holy Roman Empire, he might be hoping to do damage to us as well." Denys scratched his chin for a moment. "It is a thought, that. If he could end the truce, war would damage all parties, even if one were the victor. He could claim Germany is in no position to help England in their war with France, and thus delay his full implementation of the treaty he has with King Edward of England, and he could curry favor with Rome by drawing France into another expensive venture, thus weakening the Kingdom."

Simon grunted. "Yet the entire theory rests upon a handful of coins that could mean nothing. We need more proof."

Marcus pursed his lips then turned to Denys. "Is there any way you could get us in to see the prisoners?"

"Which ones?"

"The three young men."

Denys laughed. "I don't see how, and I fear making such inquiries could raise suspicions and implicate me even further."

Marcus sighed. "True. But—"

A messenger rushed up on horseback, cutting him off. "Are you Sir Marcus de Rancourt?"

Marcus nodded. "I am."

"I have a message." A folded paper was handed over, and the messenger disappeared as quickly as he had come.

"Who's it from?" asked Simon.

Marcus unfolded it, his eyes shooting wide. "David!"

"How did he find you?"

Marcus quickly read the letter. "It appears there was trouble, and they were forced to leave Thomas' residence."

Simon grumbled. "Where are they now?"

"At Lord Charles."

"Fools! Don't they know the risk they've put themselves in?"

Marcus was more forgiving. "They must not have had a choice. David and Jeremy are smarter than that. Come, we must make all haste." He mounted his horse, turning to Denys. "Sir, I suggest you return to your home and increase your guard. If anyone finds out you are aware of our suspicions, you could be in danger."

Denys mounted his horse and nodded. "A wise precaution. But you too must be wary. If King Adolf is involved, those acting on his behalf may have nothing to lose should they fear capture."

De Rohan Residence
Paris, Kingdom of France

Lady Joanne rushed down the steps to greet the new arrivals, Jeremy and David on her heels, Tanya beating them all, the mastiff eager to see her master once again, jumping at him in excited euphoria, the man equally pleased to see her, giving her several thumping hugs before pointing at the ground. Joanne found it remarkable how the dog obeyed every command given by this knight who had already done so much for her.

"Thank the Lord you're all right, Cousin!"

Marcus bowed deeply, Simon following. "And you, Cousin. When I received word that you were here, I was concerned." He eyed David. "I'm sure my squire has a good explanation."

David gulped. "Well, umm, sir—"

Jeremy jabbed a finger at Mrs. Thibault. "This one snuck out and had someone fetch her man, here! She nearly got us all killed!"

Marcus frowned at Thibault, standing at the top of the steps with the brick wall of a doorman they had met earlier. The fact she seemed unconcerned with what she had done, angered him greatly. "I assume he was followed by someone watching her residence?"

David nodded. "Yes, sir. We spotted him, made quick work of him and his partner, but decided we couldn't risk staying in case a third man had gone for reinforcements."

"Good thinking."

Joanne stepped closer. "*Very* good thinking. We were pursued the last several miles. Your squires bravely held them off until we were safe."

Marcus smiled, slapping both his friends on the back. "I knew I left my cousin in the right hands."

David grinned at Jeremy, both exchanging punches on the shoulder. "Told you he wouldn't be angry."

"No, you didn't."

Marcus took Joanne aside. "Your husband, have you spoken with him?"

She smiled. "Yes, all is well now. He agrees that the letter contained nothing but lies. We are again on good footing."

Marcus nodded. "I'm happy to hear that."

"And what news do you have? Has there been progress?"

"Yes, but there's little time to explain." He raised his voice so the others could hear. "Three men turned themselves in today, confessing to being the partners of the wives accused in the adultery scandal. But I believe they are lying." He stared up the steps at Thibault. "And I have a feeling you might be able to help me."

A smile revealing the start of several rotting teeth spread as she descended the steps. "I'm always pleased to be of service."

"We need to get someone into the prison to talk to these men."

"Is that all?"

"And they must speak German."

She tossed her head back, laughing. "You, my good sir, are a most fortunate man. Clearly, the good

Lord is on your side, and I'll also be on it for the right price."

He stared at her. "You dare ask for money after what you did?"

She frowned. "I suppose a little charity never hurts from time to time."

"A wise answer." Marcus dismissed the remuneration discussion with a wave of his hand. "Now, explain to me how I am most fortunate."

"I know someone who works in the kitchen at the prison, and I know for a fact that she serves the prisoners their meals."

Marcus exchanged a quick smile with Simon. "And she speaks German?"

"No, this isn't some perfect world where miracles occur just because you need them to."

Marcus frowned. "Then I fail to see how this helps us."

"And that's because you have no experience in business." She raised a finger, cutting off his response. "I also know a girl who speaks German, and she and her husband just happen to owe me money."

"How fortunate for them."

Thibault gave him a look. "Do you want my help, or do you want to continue with the insults?"

Marcus urged her on with a wave of his hand. "I apologize. Continue."

"Very well. Here's what we'll do. I'll have my girl at the prison fall ill, and my German-speaking girl will show up as her replacement. She will take over the duties, and get in to see your prisoners."

Marcus sighed. "It troubles me to no end that I must avail myself of your services, but I see that I have no choice. Arrange it."

Thibault scurried away, motioning toward her man. Marcus stepped away from the group, drawing Simon with him. A whispered conversation took place, with Simon's eyebrows rising with each sentence spoken. Joanne strained her ears to overhear what was said, yet caught nothing but mumblings.

"Make all haste, my friend," was finally heard, and Simon mounted his horse, departing immediately. Marcus rejoined the others, and Joanne approached him, lowering her voice.

"Is everything all right?"

He nodded. "Yes, just a small matter I need taken care of. Nothing to concern yourself with."

Thibault returned with her man. "We must leave at once to make the arrangements."

La Conciergerie Prison
Paris, Kingdom of France

"You're new."

Claudette kept her eyes directed at the floor, it taking everything she could manage to prevent her hands from shaking at the sight of the guards. "Yes, sir. Sabine has taken ill. I'm filling in for her until she feels better. It shouldn't be more than a day or two, I'm sure."

The guard inspected the cart loaded with the meager offerings for the prisoners, then waved her through. "I don't know why we bother feeding them. They're all going to be dead soon enough."

Claudette curtsied. "I'm sure I don't know either."

The guard waved at his partner who unlocked the door leading to a long hall, half a dozen cells on either side, the only light provided by sparsely spaced torches.

She pushed the cart through the door, her hands shaking so badly the contents rattled.

"Don't linger too close to the cells. Some of these men haven't seen a woman in years."

This sent the rattling into a frenzy. "Y-yes, sir."

She pushed the cart toward the first cell, and nearly peed when the door slammed shut behind her, leaving her alone with men who had nothing to lose. Her heart pounded, her vision blurring, as she wondered if a month's forgiven interest on her husband's loan to Mrs. Thibault was worth the risk.

The sad fact of the matter was that it was, the interest payments taking up almost every bit they managed to earn. It was a hard life, especially as refugees from Germany, their accents dead giveaways that they were foreigners. But life was hard where they had been, and when their lord had taken a liking to her, making it clear she would have to share particular…favors should she and her husband wish to continue working his land, her husband hadn't hesitated in taking action once she told him what had been said.

They left.

But not before he torched the entire homestead.

They were fugitives, hiding in a city filled with them.

And Simone Thibault had been there waiting to prey on them from the moment they arrived.

She pushed the meager offerings through the small hole at the bottom of the first cell, as she had been told to, the kitchen staff relieved that Sabine had sent her own replacement, everyone thankful they wouldn't have to cover her terrifying duties.

This Sabine woman had apparently told Thibault which cell had the new arrivals, three men of whom questions needed asking, and as she approached it, she began shaking again. She pushed three servings of bread and cheese through the opening, followed by three cups of water. She leaned closer to the bars, peering into the darkness within, then in perfect German, said, "I'm a friend."

"What did you say?"

She suppressed a smile. The response had been in German, confirming what Thibault had suspected, and guaranteeing the bonus of an extra two-month's reprieve should she prove successful. "I'm a friend. I was sent on behalf of the King to let you know that you must persevere. Help will be forthcoming."

Three shadows approached, revealing themselves to the dim torchlight as they neared the bars. "We are prepared to die for our king. There was no mention of rescue," said one.

"Plans have changed, at least that's what I was told, but there's a problem."

"What?"

"I went to meet my contact last night, and he had been arrested. Now I don't have any way of finding out what the final instructions were."

"*Scheisse*! Then we are still doomed."

Her heart was hammering, but as she continued, undiscovered, her hands trembled less, and the fear turned into excitement. "Not necessarily. Surely you have contacts on the outside. All I need is to meet with one of them, and they can find out the plan."

The man who had been doing the talking stepped closer. "This sounds like a trick."

She shook her head vehemently. "I assure you, it isn't. But if I'm to help you, I must know now, before the guard becomes suspicious. I may not be able to get in here again, then all will be lost."

The three men disappeared into the darkness, and she could hear them conferring. She continued down the cells, feeding the others, then on her way back, paused again where the three men who had confessed to the dastardly scheme were held. The leader stepped forward.

"We have no choice but to trust you, *fräulein*. Listen carefully."

De Rohan Residence
Paris, Kingdom of France

Simone Thibault had been true to her word, one young woman falling mysteriously ill before her afternoon shift in the kitchen, another showing up conveniently to take her place, a woman who had followed her instructions to the letter, and now sat before them, describing everything that had happened in exquisite detail.

"Thank you for your assistance in this matter. You are very brave."

The woman smiled shyly. "The motivation was great." She glanced at Thibault, who frowned.

"Yes, yes, three months forgiven."

The woman beamed then stood. "May I go now?"

Marcus rose, as did the others. "Yes, and again, I thank you. I must insist you tell no one of what happened, for your own safety. Not even your husband, if at all possible."

"I won't even tell my priest!"

Marcus chuckled. "You've done nothing wrong, so I'm sure it wouldn't be necessary." He motioned toward the door, and made a point of looking at Thibault. "Now, if you two would excuse us, we have private matters to discuss."

Thibault didn't appear pleased, but rose and followed the young woman out the door with her bodyguard Enzo. Simon closed the door, then they all gathered at the table.

Marcus addressed the group. "I think there can be little doubt now who is behind this."

Simon nodded. "Agreed."

"The why is also probably settled, though isn't quite as important. Now the question is how do we prove it?"

Simon motioned after the departed. "The instructions she discovered for meeting their contact are quite specific, including the time. I think that's our best course of action."

Jeremy agreed. "So, we attempt a meeting, capture their contact, and force him to confess."

Marcus smiled at him. "As good a plan as any, though we must be careful. He will certainly have someone, perhaps many, to watch his back. And remember, we have no idea if this will work. He may have no reason to be waiting for a contact attempt."

Simon leaned forward. "But isn't this the same method Mrs. Thibault used to notify him that Miss Girard was ready?"

Marcus nodded. "It is, which is why I have some confidence this may work." He turned to his squires. "You two aren't known to anyone involved as far as we know. You'll leave the message, then return here as quickly as possible. Simon and I will take up position about an hour beforehand at the rendezvous point that our traitors have indicated, and see who shows up." He turned to Thomas. "Thomas, I have a special assignment for you."

The young man beamed. "I'd be honored to help in any way I can."

"Excellent, for yours may be the most important job of all." Marcus regarded the group gathered.

"Now remember, nobody can know any of these plans. *Nobody.* You'll note I've excluded Lord and Lady Joanne, as well as Mrs. Thibault from this meeting. Only those who need to be involved know what is happening tonight. Secrecy is essential, or all could be lost. Understood?"

His men answered in unison. "Yes, sir!"

Thomas gulped. "Umm, yes, umm, sir?"

De Montfort Residence
Paris, Kingdom of France

"Are you sure we can trust him?"

Marcus eyed the heavy security now in place at Sir Denys' residence, pleased to see the man was taking their warning seriously. Lord Charles had also increased the guard, though it appeared not to the extent that now greeted them. He glanced at Simon, riding beside him. "Yes, I believe so. He's just a patsy in this."

"Are you sure?"

Marcus frowned. "I'm not sure of anything, but I believe he was being used to draw Lord Charles into the scandal to discredit him as well, so the conspirators could remove four influential members of the Court in one fell swoop."

"They should have stuck with three."

Marcus chuckled. "Perhaps. Though should we have not become involved, Lady Joanne would have been arrested, and Sir Denys shortly thereafter. She would proclaim her innocence, as the other wives would have, but no one would believe her, especially after the three men turned themselves in and the other wives were tortured into false confessions." He sighed. "Her fate would have been sealed with the others, as would his. No, I think he's perhaps the only person we *can* trust."

Sir Denys appeared surprised to see them, greeting them with a broad smile as they entered his office. Much had happened since they had last seen him at

Lord Gaspard's, and Marcus had no intention of sharing the plans now unfolding, even if he did trust him.

The fewer who knew, the better.

"Gentlemen, to what do I owe the pleasure of your company? I pray you have news?"

Marcus bowed. "None that we can share at this moment, though I do have a favor to ask of you.

"Anything."

"I'm happy to hear you say that, sir. It is my sincere belief that all will be revealed tonight. In order to see this through, however, I will need a significant contingent to make the arrests, warrants sworn out by the Court, and the Court assembled tomorrow morning so the charges and proof can be presented."

Denys' eyes were wide, his eyebrows high. "You already know who is behind this?"

Marcus raised a precautionary hand. "I have my suspicions, and am confident they will be confirmed in short order."

"Who, pray tell? I'm dying to know!"

Simon grunted. "So am I."

Marcus smiled. "Neither of you would believe me if I told you, and we cannot have them named on the warrants in case someone at the Court warns them. For now, they must be nameless warrants. I will explain everything. There is much to do, and little time."

St. Severin Church
Paris, Kingdom of France

David entered the church, an impressive affair, though nothing like he had experienced in the Holy Land. It was now evening, and a disappointing number of worshipers were present, though for their purposes, that might be a good thing.

As he went through the customary rituals, he scanned their surroundings for anything suspicious, finding nothing. He headed for the front, his eyes on the third pew, far left, sighing with relief that no one was seated there.

Time was of the essence, and a delay while waiting for some devout worshipper to finish, was not part of the plan.

He sat in the corner, Jeremy beside him, and surreptitiously stuck the note between the bench and the end of the pew requesting a meeting tonight in the gap. He bowed his head and prayed for their success, apologizing profusely to God for using His house in such a manner, and in using prayer to disguise their true purpose.

Though he was confident they would be forgiven. After all, what they were doing was for the greater good, and the lives of too many innocents were at stake.

"Let's go," he whispered, and they both rose, exiting the pew and making the sign of the cross before beating a retreat that David tried to make appear casual to any who might be watching. They

215

had no way of knowing if someone was already in the church, monitoring for a drop, though Marcus had thought it unlikely. The appointed time for a meeting was still several hours from now, and according to the instructions provided by the imprisoned accomplices, as long as a message was left at least an hour beforehand, the meeting would take place.

And there was no way someone would wait for hours for a message that may never arrive—it would appear too suspicious.

David mounted his horse, urging it forward at a reasonable pace, not wanting to draw any attention lest Marcus was wrong, all the while keeping a wary eye out for anyone suspicious. He glanced at Jeremy. "That went as well as could be expected."

"Assuming whoever is collecting it didn't spot us."

"What, you don't trust your master?"

Jeremy smiled. "Don't try and twist my words." He shook his head. "Is your heart pounding as hard as mine?"

David chuckled. "Harder. I don't think I've been this on edge since we've been in France, and there's not a sword in sight." He flicked his reins. "Let's get to the rendezvous as quickly as we can. I don't like being this exposed."

De Rohan Residence
Paris, Kingdom of France

Lady Joanne threw her arms out as she rushed toward Beatrice, her poor chambermaid leaping from her bedside, her own arms outstretched. The reunion was tearful and perhaps inappropriate for the difference in their stations, but Joanne didn't care, too relieved to worry about decorum at a moment like this.

"Thank the Lord you're all right."

Beatrice turned her head slightly to her right, nodding. "Yes, thank the Lord."

Joanne frowned, placing a finger on the woman's chin and pushing her head gently so she could see the side Beatrice was hiding. She gasped at the swollen eye revealed. "Oh my God!" She didn't bother asking who was responsible. She knew. She had heard the blow that had caused it herself. "I'm so sorry, Beatrice, I truly am."

"It's not your fault, Milady, it was my own."

"How can you possibly say that?"

"I should have ducked."

Joanne stared at her for a moment, then snickered, ashamed of herself as she struggled to stop the laugh that threatened to erupt.

Beatrice beat her to it, and they both laughed uncontrollably, the tension, the fears, the relief, the simple raw emotions causing them to react irrationally to the horrifying situation.

Joanne hugged her again. "Oh, how I've missed you." She sat Beatrice gently on the side of the bed, joining her. "Tell me, honestly, are you all right?"

Beatrice nodded. "Time will heal this. And I'm sure he would have done far worse to you." She lowered her head. "I'm just ashamed that I told him where you were."

Joanne shook her head, squeezing the poor girl's hand. "Oh, dear, you have nothing to apologize for. You saved me, and you should be proud of that."

Beatrice blushed. "Is, umm, everything all right now?"

Joanne patted the woman on the knee. "Yes, all has been forgiven. My cousin, Sir Marcus, has been able to prove that the letter was a fabrication."

"Thank God for him!"

"Yes, indeed. Now, we need to figure out who gave you the letter."

"I told them before. I'm pretty sure it must have been Albert, but I don't really remember. Everything is a jumble."

"They spoke to him, and in fact, the entire staff, and nobody remembers giving you the letter."

Beatrice's eyes widened slightly. "Oh no!" She sighed, wringing her hands. "I've been trying to remember who gave me the note, but I'm not sure. I thought it was Albert, but if he says it wasn't him, then I don't rightly know. I can't think of anyone else. I was in such a panic, I must have blocked the memory somehow."

Joanne frowned. "Then perhaps it is as they say. Someone from outside gained entry and handed it to you."

Beatrice looked up at her. "But wouldn't I remember that? Wouldn't I remember a stranger handing me a message for Lord Charles?"

Joanne nodded. "One would think, but the mind can play cruel tricks when it is under stress."

Beatrice shook her head. "But I have flashes of Albert handing me the note. In fact, I'm sure I dreamt last night that he handed it to me, saying to give this to the master, as it was most urgent. I woke up in a cold sweat with the memory."

Joanne smiled at the poor woman. "It was only a dream."

"I know, I know, but it felt so real, as if I had actually experienced it. And why was it unsealed? The seal on it had been broken. Would a messenger actually break the seal? Perhaps by accident, but surely he would have mentioned it."

"Maybe he mentioned it to Albert, but he forgot to mention it to you?"

Beatrice shrugged. "Perhaps, but when he handed it to me, I mentioned it to him, and he shrugged—oh my God! He *did* hand it to me! I remember it clearly now as if it were just moments ago. I went to say good day to him, as I do every morning."

Joanne winked. "Who's sweet on whom?"

Beatrice blushed. "He handed me the folded message. He said, 'Give this to the master, it is most urgent, I think it's about your mistress.' I said, 'Oh no, the seal is broken. How did this happen?' He shrugged, said I had better hurry, and I did. But because he had mentioned it was about you, I feared something might be wrong, so I unfolded the note, read it—thank the good Lord you taught me!—and

219

that's when I learned the nature of its contents. I hid it under the master's breakfast service, warned you, and arranged your escape with Albert."

Joanne's heart raced at the revelation. "That doesn't sound like a dream to me!"

Beatrice shook her head vigorously. "No, it isn't! I clearly remember it now."

Joanne's mind was racing. If Beatrice was correct, then Albert had lied, and she could think of no reason why. She gripped her friend by the hand. "Then the question is, why did Albert have the message in the first place, and why did he lie about it?"

"Obviously someone gave it to him," said Beatrice. "But why was the seal broken?" She stared at her mistress. "We need to find out."

Joanne rose. "You're right. We must see him right away."

Beatrice's eyes opened wide. "But the master, he said I must stay here."

Joanne batted away the statement. "Never mind him, he left a short while ago, something to do with what's been going on. We need answers, and I'm not willing to wait for his return."

Rue des Barres
Paris, Kingdom of France

"So, you're not going to tell me?"

Marcus glanced at Simon. "Tell you what?"

"Who you think is behind all this?"

Marcus shook his head. "No."

"Why not?"

He grinned at his friend. "Because if I'm wrong, I don't want you to think I'm not the genius I'm playing today."

Simon snorted. "Oh, don't worry, there's no risk of that."

"Oh?"

"No, the Lord himself couldn't convince me you're a genius."

"Touché."

Simon laughed, then became serious. "Do you think he—whoever he is—is going to show tonight?"

Marcus shrugged. "I have no idea. I'd say the chances are half-and-half. *If* the drop-off was exclusive to those three men, then no, I don't think he'll show, but the fact it was the same as where Thibault's man was instructed to notify our mystery man that Miss Girard was ready for her role as Lady Joanne, then that suggests it's used for multiple contacts. It makes sense. If we assume that this conspiracy is being coordinated by only a few, or perhaps even by only one, then having half a dozen or more contact points throughout the city would be difficult to manage. He would spend his entire time monitoring them." Marcus shook his head. "No, I think there is only one point for this entire operation, and that only one or two are actually coordinating it. And, I think, since the operation is still underway, he will still be monitoring it, especially now that they are so close to accomplishing their goal."

Simon nodded slowly. "What you say makes sense, yet without knowing who you suspect, I'll have to trust in your genius."

Marcus grinned. "So, we're back to me being a genius?"

Simon frowned. "I think the Lord and I will reserve judgment."

Rue de la Huchette
Paris, Kingdom of France

Thomas shivered in the chill of the night, the alleyway he had secreted himself in with his horse, blocking some of the wind, but the fact he had to keep his eye on a specific landmark meant he was always at least partially exposed, especially to the gusts.

He would give anything to be back at his humble home in front of the fire right now, though the fires had barely been embers of late. Once this situation was over, the luxuries provided by sheltering Mrs. Thibault would be over, and even if Sir Marcus kept his promise of giving him the coins found on the would-be assassins, they would soon run out.

Then he would be back to his life of starvation and cold.

If he continued on his current path, he would be dead before spring. He didn't fear death, though his father would have wanted more of him—would have *expected* more of him. The man would be ashamed of what he had let himself become in only a few short weeks without him.

His self-pity was killing him.

He had always managed to find some work in the past, mostly odd jobs, barely enough to provide a little help at home, but it would never be enough now that his father's meager income wasn't there to support them.

Which still left him with the two offers now available to him. One that would give him the life of a peasant, though good with the Lord, and another that would give him a life far more comfortable, though with questionable standing when Saint Peter greeted him. He sighed, his breath visible in the cold, making him painfully aware of the chill.

He shook his head, frowning, as his decision was made. And it was the only decision he *could* make, if he were to have the life he craved, and not give up his family home.

And he doubted Sir Marcus would be happy with his choice.

In fact, he was certain of it.

Yet he could see no other option.

Life toiling on a farm had never been his dream.

Rue des Barres
Paris, Kingdom of France

Simon stood in the shadows, chilled to the bone, the cold of France in the fall teeth-chattering compared to the warmth of the desert. Though it could get cold overnight as the ground gave up its heat, it was nothing compared to this.

And at least in the Holy Land, one knew come morning, the chill would rapidly dissipate, and the unbearable heat would return.

He stared at the street, his master's instructions still perplexing.

Do nothing.

Nothing? Why nothing? If the Germans' contact showed, then why weren't they going to capture him and make him talk? It made no sense to him, but then again, Marcus was a knight, and the master strategist of the group. He trusted him with his life, and would always obey the man's orders, even if they made no sense to him.

David and Jeremy had arrived on schedule, the message delivered, and now they all waited, hidden, waiting to do nothing, if things were to go according to plan. The two squires were in position with their bows, covering the streets below should something go wrong, though Marcus had indicated he expected it to be uneventful.

Nothing should be done unless lives were in danger.

Simon stamped his feet, trying to keep warm, wondering how much longer it would be before their prey was to arrive.

Prey.

He growled.

You hunt prey, you don't watch it then let it get away.

But Marcus was smart, far smarter than him. He claimed to know who was involved, which was much more than he could say for himself. He had no clue. King Adolf was probably involved, but who was acting on his behalf? He had no idea beyond those they had already killed, and the three young men who had turned themselves in to further the conspiracy.

And who was pulling the strings? He was at a loss, and that was why he couldn't understand Marcus not wanting to capture the man they hoped would be showing up any moment now.

Maybe you aren't ready to be a knight.

Horse's hooves on cobblestone echoed through the night, and he withdrew deeper into the shadows. It could be their target, or it could merely be someone passing through. The streets weren't exactly deserted at this hour, though men on horseback were indeed few, this not an area of the city known for its wealth, though it wasn't the squalor poor Thomas had grown up in.

The lone figure passed his position, a hooded cloak hiding his features, and Simon's heart rate ticked up a few notches as he realized this could indeed be the man, as most on horseback, at least those who were honest men, were usually proud to show their faces.

He peered across the street, and could see the alleyway Marcus was hiding in, but saw no evidence of him. He too was sticking to the plan, a plan that was irritating him. Their man was right there, not ten paces from him. Simon gripped the hilt of his sword, but held his place.

The man came to a stop, looking about. Nothing was said, no calls into the dark, just several snorts from the horse. There was no doubt now that this was the man they were waiting for. Simon desperately wanted to rush from his position, pull the man from his horse, and end all of this intrigue this moment.

But what if he's only a messenger?

His jaw dropped. This man could be nobody. He could simply have been sent by whoever was actually behind the conspiracy, and if they grabbed this peon now, he might tell them nothing, and all would be lost.

He smiled.

Maybe Marcus was a genius after all.

The man slowly turned in his saddle, searching the shadows, searching for his contact.

How long will he wait?

The man flicked his reins, sending his horse back in the direction he had come.

Not long, I guess.

Suddenly a horse whinnied and Marcus burst from the alleyway. "Halt!" The man glanced over his shoulder then urged his horse forward, breaking out into a gallop as Marcus gave chase. Simon cursed and rushed for his horse, tied up farther down the alleyway lest it make a noise that might tip off the man they had been waiting for. By the time he reached it and returned to the street, Marcus and their target were gone.

"What just happened?"

Simon turned to see David and Jeremy racing toward him on foot, their bows gripped uselessly in their hands. He shook his head. "I don't know. But he's on his own now."

Marcus raced after his target, urging his steed forward, and smiled as the man guided his horse to the right, exactly as he had suspected. His instructions to his men had been clear, and they had been followed.

Do nothing, unless lives are at risk.

And none were.

David and Jeremy both could have loosed an arrow to bring the man down once he had given chase, but no one's life had been in danger, and they had followed their orders.

Reluctantly, he had no doubt.

He spotted the river ahead and eased off the reins slightly, his horse a little faster than that ahead of him. He grinned as the rider crossed the bridge and it immediately began to rise.

Precisely as it had their first night in Paris.

Thomas' heart leaped as he spotted the bridge start to rise. He grabbed his horse and climbed on, watching the rider who had just crossed, race past his position. Thomas counted to three then followed, keeping his distance, the rider checking over his shoulder several times, Thomas riding high in the saddle, trying to give the man no reason to think anything untoward was happening.

The man soon eased off, apparently confident he had shaken his pursuer, and Thomas followed at a reasonable though not brisk pace. It didn't take long for the rider to reach his destination, a large estate along the River Seine, the gates swinging open for him, then closing the moment he cleared them.

Thomas stared up at the yellow and black flag flapping in the wind, unsure of what it represented, but pleased he had accomplished the task set out for him by Sir Marcus.

Now all he had to do was wait.

Marcus returned to find his sergeant and squires atop their horses in the square where he had left them, all apparently still confused by his orders, if their expressions were any indication.

"I thought our orders were to do nothing?" asked Simon as he approached.

"Yes, *your* orders were."

"Uh huh. And just where did you go off to?"

Marcus smiled. "I was merely flushing quail." He regarded his men. "Are you ready to find out who is behind this?"

Simon nodded. "Absolutely, especially if there is a fire involved. These bones are too accustomed to the desert."

Marcus laughed, turning his horse back toward the bridge. "Come, let us meet young Thomas, and see what he has found."

Jeremy rode up on his left. "Thomas? Where has he been this entire time?"

"Exactly where he needed to be."

"Which was?"

"The opposite side of the bridge."

Simon stared at him. "What bridge?" He paused. "Wait, you mean the same bridge from two nights ago? The drawbridge?"

Marcus grinned. "Now you're catching on."

"What makes you think he'd go there?"

Marcus pointed ahead, the bridge visible in the distance. "Why not? It's an arrangement he's had with the gatekeeper for some time, it's effective, and if he is who I think he is, he would have little choice but to go there."

Simon snorted. "You are mighty confident tonight, aren't you?"

Marcus grunted. "Let us pray that this confidence isn't unwarranted." He flicked his reins, hurrying back toward the bridge, praying to the good Lord that he was right about everything, otherwise he might have just let their only suspect get away.

Thomas waited in the darkness for what felt like hours, but could only have been a fraction of that, when four riders approached. He peered into the inky black and sighed with relief at the sight of Sir Marcus' white surcoat, the red cross of the Templars emblazoned across it. He urged his horse toward them, Marcus smiling.

"So, my young friend, what have you found?"

Thomas pointed at the large estate just ahead. "He went in there, sir." His eyes narrowed. "But how did you know he would? I mean, how did you know where I would be?"

Marcus smiled, pointing at the flag flying proudly at the gate. "See that flag?"

"Yes."

"Do you know what it represents?"

Thomas shook his head. "I'm afraid I don't."

"It is the flag of the Holy Roman Empire, signaling the German ambassador's residence. I spotted it when we went to see Lord Victor, and tragically discovered him murdered, likely by somebody inside this very house right now."

Simon stared at the estate. "What now?"

"Now we pray Sir Denys has been successful in his assignment, but David and Jeremy, I have another task for you."

De Rohan Residence
Paris, Kingdom of France

It had taken far longer to meet with the stable boy, Albert, than Lady Joanne had expected, the young man apparently sent off on some task earlier in the day. She had left instructions for him to be sent to Beatrice's quarters as soon as he returned, and she smiled at the eagerness in his eyes when her chambermaid opened the door to him, then the disappointed shock when he spotted his mistress sitting in the corner.

He no doubt thought he might be sharing some tender moments.

"Umm, Milady, I'm sorry, I didn't…I mean, I don't know…" He sighed, his shoulders slumping. "I was told to come here?"

She smiled. "Close the door, please."

He complied, then began to tremble.

"Sit, young one, you have nothing to fear from me, as long as you tell the truth." She pointed at the only other chair in the room, brought in for the occasion. Beatrice sat on the edge of her bed, smiling at him. "This letter to your master that you were asked of before. It was you who gave it to Beatrice, was it not?"

He vehemently shook his head. "No, Milady, it wasn't I!"

She leaned forward, putting on her most intimidating face. "I said you have nothing to fear from me as long as you told me the *truth*. Lie to me again, and I shall withdraw my promise."

His eyes bulged in fear, his entire body shaking. "Y-yes, Milady."

Joanne gestured toward Beatrice. "You like my chambermaid, do you not?"

He blushed, stealing a glance at Beatrice. "Umm, yes, Milady?"

"Do you know that she is in a great deal of trouble, and under a great deal of suspicion, because she claims you gave her the message, yet you deny it? Do you realize that if we cannot determine who gave her the letter, the Court will decide that *no one* gave it to her, and that she fabricated these lies herself? Do you know what that could mean?"

He cringed. "N-no."

"It could mean torture and imprisonment, or perhaps even death! Do you want her to die?"

Tears streamed down Beatrice's cheeks, and Joanne wasn't certain if she were merely a clever actress, or if she were genuinely afraid, now that the unspoken truth had finally been voiced.

"Tell me who gave you the message, or she dies!"

And when Albert finally revealed the truth, she nearly fainted.

233

Approaching the German Ambassador's Residence
Paris, Kingdom of France

Sir Denys rode at the head of a far smaller column of the King's Personal Guard than he would have hoped, half a dozen men all that the Court could provide on such short notice, the request made of the King in his chambers, and surprisingly approved.

It would appear the monarch was eager to uncover the truth as well, a surprising sense of relief rushing through Denys in the discovery, as part of him had feared that perhaps the King could be involved, if only tacitly.

Though for the moment, nothing appeared further from the truth.

To say he had been stunned when told hours ago where he was to bring the soldiers and the warrants, would be an understatement. Despite his pleas for an explanation, none had been provided him, making his task even more difficult.

Though he had succeeded. He had the unnamed warrants in his pocket, and stunningly, the Court was convening at this very moment, the King unwilling to wait until morning to find out what was afoot. He just prayed that Sir Marcus was prepared for this eventuality, as it was the one part of his instructions he hadn't fulfilled to the Templar's exact specifications.

As they approached the German ambassador's residence, he peered into the darkness, searching for Marcus, and breathed a heavy sigh of relief as he spotted the white surcoat against the moonlight reflecting off the waters of the River Seine.

Marcus and Simon, along with another young man, approached on horseback, and he brought the column to a halt.

"I see you were successful in your task," said Marcus.

Denys nodded. "Not without some difficulty, and not in the numbers I had hoped."

"No matter. The warrants?"

Denys patted his breast pocket. "Secured as requested, though one thing didn't, unfortunately, go according to plan."

"Oh?"

"The Court is assembling *now*. The King was unwilling to wait until morning."

Marcus chuckled. "I suspected that might happen. It is of no concern." He motioned toward the residence. "Once we pass through those gates, I will have confirmed everything, and you will be able to put names on those warrants."

Denys eyed the impressive walls. "You intend to enter by force?"

"If necessary."

Denys glanced at his too few men. "I don't think we have enough, should they resist."

Marcus smiled. "That is why I sent my sergeant on a little errand earlier today." He placed his fingers to his lips and whistled. The sounds of a large contingent on horseback was heard in the distance, approaching from the opposite direction, and Denys' eyes bulged as dozens of white surcoats with red crosses became visible. Marcus smiled. "As you can see, I brought some friends, just in case."

German Ambassador's Residence
Paris, Kingdom of France

"You were a fool to come here!"

German Ambassador Gerhardt von Brunswick glared at his visitor as the man removed the cloak that had disguised him.

"Where else was I to go? He was in pursuit. Besides, he has no clue who I am, and I lost him at the bridge, just like last time."

Gerhardt shook his head as his heart pounded with rage. Two nights ago, when his partner in this affair had arrived under similar circumstances, he had ordered him never to do it again, yet here he stood. "You broke your word."

"I had no choice. This is closer than my home, and as I did last time, I felt it was best to get off the streets as quickly as possible. I'll stay for only a short while, and leave as if I were visiting a friend."

"We are *not* friends." Gerhardt returned to his chair behind his desk, trying to calm himself, his leg always hurting when filled with rage. This man might not be a friend, but he was buried up to his neck with him in the affair he now found himself in. Approached several months ago with a proposal that could benefit Germany, he had listened with great interest at the idea of manipulating the membership of the King's Court to foment war with Flanders, thus allowing Germany to ease out of its treaty with England that was proving to be a disadvantage.

The man had been well-informed, and had impeccable credentials as a senior member of the Court.

Gerhardt had requested instructions from King Adolf, and had been ordered to proceed, a substantial amount of funds forwarded to accomplish the task.

All that his partner had requested was a significant payment upon completion, and absolutely no recognition from King Adolf, should he succeed.

His identity was to be kept a complete secret, and in fact, only Gerhardt knew who he was.

And only this man knew Gerhardt was involved. His capture could compromise them all.

"I want you out of here, now! I can't risk you being caught!"

His partner frowned. "There's more chance of that should I leave now." He dropped into a chair. "My friend, you must learn to remain calm in these situations. There's nothing to fear."

A knock at the door sent Gerhardt's pulse racing even harder. "Come!"

The door opened and his butler entered, his eyes wide with uncharacteristic nerves.

"Yes, what is it?"

"Ambassador, I'm afraid I have most disturbing news. The King's Personal Guard, and a substantial contingent of Templar Knights, are at the front gate, demanding that you and your guest come with them at once."

Gerhardt slumped in his chair, feeling faint, as his heart threatened to explode. He glared at the instrument of his destruction sitting across from him. "You fool! You've killed us all!"

The man shook his head, raising a hand. "Did they ask for me by name?"

"Yes, Lord Charles, they did."

De Rohan Residence
Paris, Kingdom of France

"I can't believe my husband gave you the message! That means…" Joanne shook her head, struggling to stay focused as she grew faint with the shock. She sucked in a deep, unladylike breath, regaining some control. She stared at Beatrice. "What does that mean?"

"I think it means that he wrote the message, doesn't it?"

Joanne nodded vigorously. "Yes, of course, but why? What does it all mean?" She thought for a moment. Her husband had obviously written the message to himself, pretending to be someone else. He had given it to Albert, with strict instructions to give it to Beatrice and never tell anyone he had done so. Her eyes shot wide. "Wait, was the seal broken when he gave it to you?"

Albert shook his head. "Not at first. He broke it himself before handing it to me."

Joanne tapped a finger rapidly on her knee. "Then that explains that. He told you to tell Beatrice that it was about me, and broke the seal to give her the opportunity to read the message, as he knew she would be unable to resist the urge as she is loyal to me, not him." She threw her hands up in frustration.

"But why do this at all?" asked Beatrice, her cheeks burning with emotion. "Why not just let you be arrested with the rest?"

Joanne jabbed at the air with her finger as the pieces began to fall into place with this new key bit of information. "Because we now know that an imposter had been hired to impersonate me. If I fled, which he knew I would, as this was the purpose of having you read the letter he had forged, it would make me appear guilty in the eyes of the Court. Then when his guards caught me, they probably would have killed me, rather than bring me back to Paris, and there would be no need for a trial!"

"I can't believe he would do such a thing, Milady! His own wife!"

Joanne frowned, debating whether she should reveal what she knew. She sighed, there no point in protecting the honor of a man who would have her killed. "Things haven't exactly been happy these past few years. Have you not noticed the cutbacks? We've had to lay off many of our staff, we stable fewer horses than we ever have, and the meals are leaner."

Beatrice blushed, eying the floor as Albert looked away. "Yes, Milady, we have noticed that, I mean, the staff have, but none would dare say anything."

"Of course you wouldn't. But you might as well know now that we are nearly broke. My husband lost most of our money through several unwise investments and a horrendous gambling habit. It cost us some of our lands we relied upon for revenues. I fear if something drastic doesn't change, we will be forced to rely on the charity of others before long."

The door to Beatrice's room burst open, and Louis Forbin, the captain of her husband's guard, stepped inside, his thigh bandaged, his brow covered in sweat from the effort. He appeared to pose little threat, though the two men standing behind him suffered from no such afflictions.

"Albert, my boy, you were given specific instructions not to see Miss Beatrice."

Albert paled to the point of blending in with the whitewashed wall lit by candlelight and fire. "I-I'm sorry, I didn't know. I was summoned by, umm…"

Joanne rose. "He was summoned by me. And what gives you the right to enter these chambers unannounced?"

Forbin sneered at her, his contempt clear. "My master does."

"Well, I am your mistress, and I order you to return to your station."

Forbin laughed. "I'm afraid I don't take my orders from you, Milady, only from your husband."

Outside the German Ambassador's Residence
Paris, Kingdom of France

Marcus suppressed a sigh of relief in being right, and a smile at the shocked look on Sir Denys' face, as the German ambassador stepped through the gates, along with Lord Charles. Simon and the others exchanged muttered comments, obviously as stunned as Denys.

"Lord Charles! I-I don't understand! What is happening here? Why are you here?" Denys turned to Marcus. "I don't understand!"

"Neither do I!" growled Charles, his eyes wide with rage. "What is the meaning of this? You have no right!"

Marcus stared at him. "If you'll give me just a moment, Milord." He turned to Denys. "All will be explained in the Court, but for now, please complete your warrants to include the names of the German ambassador, Lord Charles de Rohan, and Louis Forbin, the captain of his personal guard. Please send some of your guards to arrest him at once. You will find him at Lord Charles' residence, recovering from a wound one of my men inflicted upon him two days ago."

Denys completed the warrants, shaking his head in apparent disbelief at the events still unfolding. He handed the first to one of the soldiers with him. "Take three men with you and bring him to the Court."

Marcus approached the soldier. "You should find my squires there as well, David and Jeremy. Have them, Lady Joanne, her chambermaid, Mrs. Thibault, and her man Enzo, join us at the Court."

"Yes, sir." The man bowed slightly in his saddle, then turned with three of his men, charging into the darkness.

Denys stared at Charles. "Why did you do it?"

"I did nothing. You will all pay dearly for this."

Marcus held up a hand. "Lord Charles, save your arguments for the King's Court. I understand His Majesty awaits us, and I'm certain he is not a man who likes to be kept waiting, especially at this hour."

244

Outside the de Rohan Residence
Paris, Kingdom of France

"Is that Tanya?"

Jeremy cocked an ear then nodded. "I'd recognize that bark anywhere. Something's wrong."

David urged his horse toward the gates of the de Rohan estate, the reinforced heavy wood doors closed. "Open the gates! It's Jeremy and David, Sir Marcus de Rancourt's squires!"

There was no reply, though David could hear activity on the other side. He didn't wait, instead dismounting then leaping at the gate, shoving upward with his left foot, gaining enough height to grab the top. Jeremy pushed David's feet from below, and he swung over, dropping to the ground and drawing his sword as the two shocked guards stood staring at him, unsure of what to do. He reached back and shoved the latch aside, kicking the gate partway open, Jeremy taking care of the rest, joining him with his bow at the ready.

"Where is Lady Joanne?" demanded David, aiming the tip of his sword at the nearest guard's throat.

"She's under arrest, by order of Lord Charles!"

David glared at him. "That's *not* what I asked."

"There!"

David looked to where Jeremy was pointing, and spotted Lady Joanne and her chambermaid being shoved across the courtyard by several of the guards, one he recognized as the Captain of the Guard they

245

had wounded in Crécy-la-Chapelle. He glanced at Tanya to his right, still tied up from where he had left her earlier, the dog straining against her leash, desperate to get involved.

And she was exactly the distraction they needed, as the two guards at the gate finally drew their swords. Jeremy buried an arrow deep in his man's chest as David swung, opening the belly of his before the man's sword cleared its scabbard. David surged forward, toward Tanya, and swung his sword, slicing her leash. She leaped forward, tearing toward those who would threaten the women, as Jeremy let fly another arrow, dropping one of the guards before they took notice of their arrival.

Tanya reached them before another arrow could be shot, taking down another guard, leaving only the captain. He spun toward them, his sword at the ready, then turned to swing at Tanya.

"No!" Jeremy let two arrows fly in quick succession, dropping the man in his place, his sword clattering to the cobblestone as he collapsed to his knees.

"Kill them!" he cried before his voice turned into a gurgle, blood sputtering from between his lips.

David turned slowly in a circle, Jeremy pressed to his back as Tanya continued to grapple with her prey. Half a dozen of Charles' guards encircled them, swords drawn, another half-dozen staff with pitchforks joining them. David reached out and grabbed Lady Joanne, pulling her then Beatrice toward him, placing them between him and Jeremy.

"Now stop right there! If you come any closer, I promise you death, though not necessarily a swift one!"

One of them laughed, the others joining in. "We're twelve, you're two."

David smiled. "I'm happy to see you can count." He pointed at the man. "Tanya! Get him!"

Tanya looked up, then to where he was pointing, releasing the mangled arm she had been tearing at, then bolted toward her new target. Jeremy put an arrow in the shoulder of the nearest guard as all were distracted by Tanya's charge. She leaped through the air and the man dropped his sword, raising his arms to protect his face. The mastiff slammed into him, bringing him to the ground, the snarling beast a terror to behold.

"Tanya! Get him!" David pointed at the next nearest guard, and she released, sailing through the air at him.

"What goes on here!"

David swung toward the new voice, and breathed a sigh of relief as four of the King's Personal Guard rode through the gate, their swords drawn. "Tanya!" David smacked his leg and the dog broke her grip, returning to his side, panting happily. He stepped toward the new arrivals.

"I am David, this is Jeremy. We were sent here by our master and Templar Knight, Sir Marcus de Rancourt. This woman, Lady Joanne, is under our protection. These men were accosting her when we arrived."

The captain of the new arrivals leaned forward in his saddle. "You said Sir Marcus de Rancourt?"

"Yes."

"We were sent here by him to arrest Louis Forbin. Where is he?"

David pointed at the body. "I think this is him."

Lady Joanne stepped forward. "It is. These two brave men and their faithful companion saved us from whatever fate my corrupt husband had in store for us."

"Your husband is Lord Charles?"

She nodded. "Yes."

"Then you need not fear him any longer. We arrested him a short time ago. I have orders to bring you to the Court immediately. The King awaits."

David bowed slightly. "We shall, but first we have one more task."

Palais de la Cité
Paris, Kingdom of France

Sir Marcus walked across the polished marble floor, thinking back on the first time he had been here, under arrest, his sergeant and at least a dozen Templars charging in on horseback. It was a sight to behold, and that day had been a shock to all those fortunate enough to have been attending the Court that day.

Yet though this was late evening, it appeared even more were here, garb from the realms of Europe and beyond, standing to the sides as the accused and witnesses were led into the massive chamber, King Philip IV seated on his throne at the far end, ceremonial guards on either side.

Marcus had addressed these people twice now, yet this time he felt insecure, too much of what he was about to say requiring those present to believe him, rather than rely upon physical evidence and confessions. Charles had proclaimed his innocence, but would he continue, once Marcus laid out his case?

King Philip rose, and the entire Court went silent. "Sir Marcus. Once again, you grace us with your presence. I understand you have some information that could prove of interest to us?"

Marcus advanced and bowed with a flourish, knowing the vanity of this man demanded observation of all the niceties expected by royalty. "I do, Your Majesty. If you will indulge me, I will explain everything."

King Philip nodded then returned to his seat. "Proceed."

"Thank you, Your Majesty." Marcus stepped to the side, motioning toward Lady Joanne. "Two days ago, Lady Joanne, my cousin through the marriage of my sister, arrived at my residence in Crécy-la-Chapelle, pursued by agents of her husband, who had accused her of adultery. After a *discussion*"—chuckles rippled through the Court, word apparently out on the details of the discussion—"it was agreed that they would return to Paris, and I would follow shortly to meet with their master to discuss the matter. Lady Joanne swore to me that she was innocent of the charges, and I believed her, however I felt the only way justice could be served, was to meet with her husband, Lord Charles.

"My sergeant and I"—Simon bowed slightly—"left immediately for Paris, and met with Lord Charles that very evening. We were informed that he had received a letter accusing her of adultery with Sir Denys de Montfort"—Sir Denys stepped forward, bowing with a flourish before retreating—"and that he was determined to seek justice. I convinced him to let me look into the matter, as she swore she was innocent. My only promise to him was that whatever I found, even if it were proof of her guilt, I would share with him. In exchange, he promised to not send anyone else after his wife, who was safely ensconced on my farm with two of my squires." David and Jeremy bowed awkwardly. Marcus turned to Lord Charles. "Sir, do you agree with everything I have said so far."

Charles glared at him, but nodded. "Of the things discussed in my presence, yes. What happened between you and my wife, I cannot."

Marcus bowed slightly. "Of course." He turned to Joanne. "And you, Milady, will you corroborate the portion of my story that involves you?"

She stepped forward. "I do."

"Thank you." Marcus turned back to address the Court. "We then visited with Sir Denys, who did not deny the affair, but some doubt was raised as to the identity of the woman he was having the affair with."

King Philip raised his hand slightly. "Excuse us? What do you mean? How could there be any confusion?"

Marcus bowed, the King clearly intrigued, noting that the monarch was sitting on the edge of his seat. "Sir Denys had commissioned a portrait of himself and who he *thought* was Lady Joanne, unbeknownst to her. It was on display when we arrived, as he was to present her with it that very evening. What was unusual was that the woman in the portrait bore little resemblance to the woman I had just met at my farm earlier that day. So little, in fact, that I was certain they were two different people."

"Perhaps the artist was better suited to painting landscapes!" shouted someone from the periphery.

Laughter filled the room and Marcus smiled, holding up a hand to gently silence them. "Perhaps, though the likeness of Sir Denys was quite excellent. Regardless of the quality of the artist's work, we met with the woman he was having the affair with, and she soon admitted she was indeed *not* the Lady Joanne."

He paused for effect, and it succeeded, gasps erupting, even King Philip leaning back in his throne, his eyes wide. Marcus let things settle down slightly before pressing on. "In fact, her name was Miss Melanie Girard, and she had been hired to impersonate Lady Joanne."

"What proof do you have?" asked someone. "Where is this woman?"

Marcus frowned. "Unfortunately, the woman was murdered."

"Then all we have is your word for it?"

Marcus shook his head. "No, there were witnesses to her confession."

"Then bring them forward."

Marcus spun on Charles, holding out his hand, palm open. "Here stands one of the witnesses." He stepped closer. "Do you confirm that you indeed met Miss Girard, and that she confessed to impersonating your wife?"

He sighed. "Yes, yes I do. But none of this points to my involvement in any way! I'm innocent—"

Marcus held up a hand. "We'll get to that. But you admit that your wife is innocent in the matter of this affair?"

He nodded. "I do."

Marcus turned to Sir Denys. "And you, sir, confirm that the woman you were led to believe was Lady Joanne, is not in fact, this lady?" He pointed at Joanne.

"I do."

Marcus turned toward the Court. "So, we have now established the innocence of Lady Joanne,

252

accused yesterday in this very Court of adultery. I think we can all agree on that?"

Nods and murmurs encircled the Court, but more importantly, the King nodded. Marcus bowed deeply to him, in case anyone watching the proceedings had missed his acknowledgment. "I thank you, Your Majesty, for agreeing that this poor woman is innocent of these most horrific charges."

The King nodded again, Marcus detecting a hint of annoyance at having been forced into what might have been a premature pardon.

Joanne nearly collapsed with relief, tears flowing down her face as she sought comfort in the arms of her chambermaid. Marcus suppressed a smile at the satisfaction in knowing he had at least succeeded in his original mission of saving his cousin, and proving her innocence.

But he wasn't done.

"Yet that was not all that happened that day," he continued. "Three other women were accused of the same crime, and the next day, these three men"—he pointed at the Germans who had already been waiting when his entourage had arrived—"turned themselves in, confessing to the crime, and claiming they had been hired by the husbands to impregnate their wives, as they had no male heirs." Another wave of indignation and disgust made its presence known. "I found this story to be ridiculous at the least, but what I couldn't understand was why they had turned themselves in. Why not flee? Perhaps if they had declared their love for these women, and begged the Court for leniency on the part of the women they loved, I could understand their actions. But they didn't. Instead, they told this ridiculous story.

"I decided to meet with one of the accused men, Lord Gaspard de Laval, and he confirmed with me that while he had no sons, unbeknownst to most, he had a brother who would inherit should anything happen to him, which didn't match the information I had previously heard." He stepped toward the three imprisoned wives. "Which of you is Lady de Laval?"

A woman stepped forward, her chin held high. "I am."

"And when you were forced to sign your confession, did you inform them that your husband had a male heir?"

"I did."

"And what was the reaction."

She glanced over at the prosecutor, whom Marcus was surprised had remained silent this entire time, only the King, he was sure, able to keep the man's mouth shut. "He seemed surprised, then amended my *confession* to include mention of my husband desiring an heir from his direct lineage."

Marcus bowed to her. "Thank you, Milady." He turned back to the court. "Obviously, these confessions were based upon the lies told by these three men"—he motioned toward the three Germans—"who obviously didn't know about the male heir Lord Gaspard had. If one of them were indeed having an affair with his wife, with her knowing full well why, then surely it would have been mentioned long before the arrest, and he would have told the prosecutor that his situation was unique." He turned to the prosecutor, now beet red. "Did he?"

The man glanced at the King whose eyes flared slightly. He turned back to Marcus. "No, he did not."

"Thank you." Marcus faced the three Germans. "Yet more holes poked into the accusations made by these three men." Marcus turned back to the crowd. "But more was going on here, and it ties back to the celebrations for the canonization of Louis IX on August ninth of this year. I'm sure you all remember the tragic stage collapse?" Assent swept the room. "Many were injured that day, and many required the use of a cane for weeks, and some still do to this day. Why is this significant, you might ask? It is for one reason. The man who hired Miss Girard to impersonate Lady Joanne, did so shortly after the stage collapse, and employed a cane. In later encounters, he did not."

"Encounters with whom?"

Marcus bowed slightly toward the side of the room the question had come from. "I'm glad you asked." He motioned toward Simone. "Mrs. Thibault is a woman of many talents in her neighborhood, known to be able to provide all manner of services. She was approached several months ago by a man who employed a cane. He had need of a woman, his description matching that of Lady Joanne, but more importantly, she needed to be trained to act like a lady. Miss Girard was hired, trained, and a month later, contact was made once again with this mysterious stranger." He beckoned Thibault. "Madam, if you would, please tell the Court how contact was made."

She stepped forward, curtseying awkwardly. "A note was left in the far left of the third pew in the St. Severin Church. The very next day, the man returned to my premises to provide final payment. I gave him the address of the girl, and a coachman that could be relied upon. I never saw him again until yesterday when he tried to kill me."

"Did you ever see his face?"

She shook her head. "No."

"Then how do you know it was the same man?"

"I'm no fool, sir. I can recognize a voice."

Laughter greeted her answer, and Marcus smiled. "Of course you can. And tell me, did he have a cane in your last encounter?"

"No."

"And before?"

"Yes, both times I met with him, he had a cane."

"But that was over two months ago."

She nodded. "Yes."

"And the man I encountered in your office yesterday, the man who tried to kill you, was quite spry, definitely not requiring a cane. That suggests, ladies and gentlemen, someone who had been injured, and had healed between these encounters."

Nods of agreement flowed throughout the room.

"Now you may ask why this is important. It is important because if we assume this man was injured in the stage collapse, which I realize is a bit of a leap at the moment, but I will fill in the gaps for you shortly, then we have a very narrow list of suspects, for as I'm sure you remember, that was the Royal stage, by invitation only." He pulled the list of names from his pocket, holding the pages in the air. "This is the list of everyone who was on the stage that day, and if we assume our suspect was injured that same day, then his name is among those listed."

A hint of nervousness flowed through the crowd, as many realized they were now suspects.

"But why is this important? How could I know that he was on the stage? The answer is, I couldn't." He held up a finger. "Not at first. It was the late Lord Victor de Courtenay who had turned me onto the idea. This brave soul introduced himself to me after I addressed the Court yesterday, proclaiming Lady Joanne's innocence. He warned me to be careful, as he suspected something more than simple adultery was afoot here. For you see, he had made a connection that I was not aware of." He paused, turning slowly so all in the room could see his face. "Have you not asked yourselves why *these* four women?"

The room leaned forward, silent, awaiting the answer.

"*All* four of the wives accused, had husbands who supported the treaty between France and Flanders."

The Court erupted in indignation and shock, arguments breaking out among what were clearly two opposing sides—outrage by those who apparently supported the truce, and righteous indignation by those who didn't. Marcus remained silent, welcoming the break, the opportunity used to collect his thoughts.

The King raised a hand, and the Court soon fell silent. "Continue, Sir Marcus."

Marcus bowed. "Thank you, Your Majesty." He turned back to those gathered. "The connection pointed out to me by Lord Victor was a shock, and simply too much of a coincidence for me to believe he

257

wasn't on to something. I noted that he employed a cane, and he related the story of the stage collapse, something I had been unaware of. He then agreed to supply me with the list of the attendees. As you know, he was murdered yesterday, before we could meet, but he was clever and brave enough to hide the list on his horse before being accosted by persons unknown. The list was retrieved, this list"—he shook the pages—"and I think the fact he was murdered suggests that he was correct in his theory."

He paused, wishing he had something to drink, his mouth going dry. But to stop now and ask, would break his momentum, and he was as eager to reveal the whole truth as he was to leave where he had no place being. "It has been explained to me by people *far* smarter than I, that should these four influential men be removed from the Court, opinion would sway in favor of those who opposed the treaty."

Outrage threatened to break out again, but Marcus raised his hand. "Please, bear with me. I too cannot think of why anyone here would want war, which is why I continued to ask questions. When accosted by two men, we found these on their persons." He held out his hand, and Simon stepped forward with the two purses taken from the men who had followed them to Thomas Durant's home. Marcus extracted several of the German coins, and presented them to the King. "These German coins were found on the men that accosted us. So, I would ask, why would two common thieves have German coins on them?"

He paused, no one saying anything as the King examined the coins, before returning them. "They are indeed German."

Marcus bowed. "Thank you, Your Majesty." He held them up, pinched between his fingers, turning to the others. "I ask again, why would two common thieves have German coins on them? And the answer is that they wouldn't, and that they weren't common thieves! They were following us, trying to find Lady Joanne. It was my belief that their orders were to find her and kill her, so that no one would be able to make the connection that she wasn't Miss Girard, who by this time was also dead, killed by an assassin's arrow. I pursued her murderer, but he escaped, having an arrangement with the gatekeeper at one of the bridges across the River Seine. He raised the drawbridge before I could overtake him, and escaped to the other side."

He clenched the coins in his fist, shaking it. "These coins led me to believe that perhaps the Germans were involved. Certainly, King Adolf might benefit if war were to break out. Both France and Flanders, and their ally England, would be poorer for it, and the weakening of England, Germany's new ally, could allow King Adolf to renege on his new treaty, the terms of which I have been informed he hasn't been meeting."

Murmured agreement filled the room, and the German ambassador shifted his weight from one foot to the other. Marcus suppressed a sigh of relief at the lack of any challenges, none of the politics he had spoken of things he was familiar with, and nothing truly corroborated—he had relied on the honesty and knowledge of those who had shared their wisdom.

"But this wasn't enough proof. Not a few coins. We needed more. And when these three men presented themselves to the Court, I knew this was the opportunity we had been looking for. I could think of no reason why these men would turn themselves in, except loyalty, loyalty to one's king, perhaps." He bowed at King Philip, who acknowledged him with a slight raising of his right hand. "And if the Germans were involved, then these men too must be German. This time, it was I who employed the services of Mrs. Thibault, who had contacts within the prison kitchen, and knew a young woman who spoke German. A convenient illness was arranged, our young lady was sent to fill the vacancy, and she was allowed into the cells when the daily meal was served. She spoke to the three prisoners in their cells, and she did so in *German*. And was responded to in kind."

Gasps then outrage erupted, the outright screams of indignity aimed at the German ambassador, overwhelming. Even the King's cheeks were red, his eyes aimed like daggers at the man, suggesting to Marcus that these revelations were as shocking to the monarch as they were to his advisors.

Perhaps this time you indeed aren't involved.

The King finally settled himself, and silenced the others by raising his hand, though it still took some time.

Marcus finally was able to continue. "This clever girl convinced these men"—he again pointed at the three accused, now appearing very uncomfortable—"to provide her with their method of contact for whoever was behind this. She provided us with this information, and should it become necessary, this brave girl can be brought to the Court, though I don't think it will be." He approached Mrs. Thibault. "What was stunning about what was revealed, was that the exact same method that Mrs. Thibault employed to contact her client, was used by these men to contact their German representative. A note, left at the left-hand corner of the third pew of the St. Severin Church. At this point, I was quite confident the Germans were involved, which likely meant the German ambassador. What I couldn't prove was who was his accomplice, for I was certain this man"—he motioned toward Gerhardt—"a rather elderly gentleman, wasn't who I chased along the River Seine that first night." Marcus smiled. "So I set a trap."

This excited those gathered, and he noted that over the past several moments, the members of the Court and their guests, had slowly closed in on those involved, rather than risk missing a word spoken. His confidence in speaking to this crowd was growing, but he still had succeeded in nothing beyond securing Lady Joanne's freedom. He had yet to *prove* anything.

"I had a message left in the church, in the far left of the third pew, requesting a meeting this very evening. We waited where these men said they would normally meet their contact after a request was made, and at the appointed hour, a rider did appear. I gave chase, but not so as to capture him, but to have him lead me to the German ambassador's residence. He again employed the drawbridge as his method of escape, and I let him, but I had positioned one of my trusted friends"—he motioned toward Thomas Durant, who blushed, diverting his eyes to his shoes—"on the other side. He followed the rider to the ambassador's residence, and we met him there."

He turned, facing Lord Charles, and slowly walked toward him as he spoke. "I had already arranged for Sir Denys to bring the King's Personal Guard with arrest warrants, and we apprehended the German ambassador and his accomplice, Lord Charles."

Charles glared at him as he no doubt tried to ignore the outrage expressed around them. Marcus met his stare, closing the gap to within a few paces. Something was thrown, hitting Gerhardt in the back of the head, causing the man to stumble forward, wincing in pain. The crowd grew quiet as the King apparently had enough, likely wanting to hear what was about to be said.

Marcus stopped his advance, eying his adversary. "Do you deny being in league with the German ambassador to undermine the truce between France and Flanders?"

Charles smiled slightly. "Yes, I do. I was merely visiting my friend when you arrived. This entire thing is preposterous. You have yet to offer one shred of proof that I am involved in this matter."

Marcus smiled. "I had a feeling you would say that." He pulled out the message given to Lord Charles, revealing the adulterous affair between his wife and Sir Denys. "Do you recognize this letter, sir?"

Charles glanced at it. "I do."

"And who gave it to you?"

"We have yet to determine that. My staff is looking into it."

"He gave it to me, sir!"

Marcus' eyebrows shot up and he turned toward the voice, a young man, poorly clad, his limbs drawn inward as if trying to make himself as small as possible. "And you are?"

"Albert, sir. I'm the stable boy."

Beatrice put an arm on his shoulder, and the boy beamed at her, his posture improving slightly at the bolstered confidence.

Marcus stepped closer. "And what did you just say?"

The boy pointed at Charles. "He gave it to me to give to Beatrice. He made me swear not to tell anyone, but, well, when I realized the lady could be executed for what was in it, I couldn't keep the secret any longer."

"You lying bastard! I'll have your head for this!"

The young boy cringed then darted behind Simon, who took a deep breath, expanding his impressive size even further.

Marcus held up the letter in one hand, then the list of names from the stage collapse in the other. "Then I suppose there's little point of noting that the handwriting is quite similar to the notes you made on these pages for me."

He beckoned David who rushed forward with a sheaf of papers. "Master David, please tell me where you acquired these papers."

"In Lord Charles' office just before we came here."

"Thank you." He turned to Thomas. "Master Thomas, please join me." Thomas' eyes bulged, but he stepped forward.

"Yes, sir?"

"You were raised by an expert in forgery, and I suspect you have an eye for such things. Do you think

263

the hand that wrote these pages, retrieved by my squire David this very hour from Lord Charles' office, was the same as the hand that wrote this letter?"

Thomas took the pages with trembling hands, holding them up to the light of a nearby torch, then nodded. "Yes, I do. Whoever wrote all of these is clearly left-handed, and the slant is identical. And the way he makes several of his letters are consistent."

Marcus smiled broadly, patting the young man on the back as he returned the pages. "Thank you, Master Thomas." Thomas quickly retreated to join the others, and Marcus stepped over to Beatrice, frowning at the swollen right eye. "You'll note, that this poor woman bears the angry mark of a man who punched her in the right eye. If one were to use the right hand to deliver such a blow, then it would be the *left* eye that would have been struck. Who gave you this wound?"

Beatrice glared at Charles. "The master did, sir."

Marcus walked toward Charles. "Can I assume you will do the honorable thing and admit that you, in fact, wrote the note to yourself, implicating your wife in an adulteress affair?"

Charles glared at him, but Marcus could tell the fight was out of him the moment the stable boy spoke. And what was remarkable about the boy's few words, was that they were more effective and damaging than anything Marcus had said up to this point.

And he had known nothing about it, though someone must have, as he hadn't asked for the boy to be brought here.

I suspect Lady Joanne is behind this.

Suddenly Charles' shoulders slumped and his face sagged as he lowered his head. "Yes," he murmured.

"Charles, no!" cried Gerhardt, rushing toward him. Simon drew his sword, cutting off his advance.

"So, you admit that you were behind all of this?"

Charles sighed, his eyes red and filled with tears that threatened to escape. "Yes, though not for the reasons you might think. When I was injured in the stage collapse, along with the German ambassador and many others, he and I helped each other, and became friends. He spoke to me of the truce, and how he felt my position on it was wrong. It was his belief, and he soon persuaded me of the same, that allowing Flanders and England to prepare for an inevitable war was unwise. He felt we should press our advantage, and claim victory before they could strengthen their defenses. I eventually agreed with his position, and what was at first a casual conversation about who would need to be swayed to change the opinion of the Court, quickly turned to outright planning for how to achieve our goal.

"It was during these discussions that I recognized an opportunity. For while I now agreed that war was ultimately best for France, as I felt she could easily win, I also had problems of my own." He stole a glance at his wife, who stared back with none of the sympathy he may have been seeking. "I was nearly bankrupt. When I suggested to the ambassador that I could handle everything, he agreed, and a substantial reward was settled upon should I succeed. It was a way out of my financial woes, with no harm coming to the Kingdom, as I truly do feel the truce is a mistake, and we could easily be victorious."

"But why did you implicate your wife in this?"

Charles shifted his weight back and forth for a moment, clearly ashamed of what he was about to say. "If I suddenly came into a lot of money, and our situation dramatically improved, she would ask questions. No matter how altruistic I feel my actions are, some might still consider it treasonous to act with the Germans in this matter."

"And you'd be right!" shouted someone, roars of agreement from the periphery erupting.

Marcus raised a hand, silencing them. "Please, sir, continue."

"Well, things hadn't been going well with my wife, so I felt by implicating her along with the others we felt needed to be removed, she would be imprisoned long enough for me to plausibly turn things around. I would then press for her release, and it would be granted, I was sure, as I was a victim."

"Yet the other three men were accused of much more than you."

"Yes. They had to be removed, as there would be no convincing them to change their minds. And we needed the charges to be so morally reprehensible, that punishment would be swift and final. But I, on the other hand, had already changed my position. When I would eventually forward my new position of opposing the treaty, my motivations wouldn't be questioned, and I might even be given a sympathetic ear after what had happened. And even if I was shunned for not controlling my wife, Gerhardt and I were convinced that those who opposed the truce would recognize the opportunity regardless, and press their advantage. We would have war, France would win without risking much, I would have my reward, and we would all move on as if nothing had happened."

"Except that three innocent husbands and their wives, would be likely imprisoned or worse."

Charles' head sagged. "Yes, but sometimes in war, the innocent die."

Marcus took the opportunity, now that a key word had been said. "So, you are admitting then, that these three men"—he motioned toward the Germans—"are liars and co-conspirators, and that these women are innocent of the crimes they have been accused of, and so are their husbands?"

Charles nodded. "Yes." He turned to the still shackled husbands and wives. "I'm so sorry for this. I-I was desperate."

"I'll see you burned at the stake for this, Charles!" shouted Lord Gaspard, his eyes filled with rage.

Marcus turned to the King. "Your Majesty, I think we can—"

The King raised a hand, cutting him off, then gestured toward the prisoners. "Free them."

Marcus bowed deeply once again. "Thank you, Your Majesty." He turned to address the Court as the husbands and wives were unshackled, tearful reunions warming his heart. "And with the last of the innocents now free, I think my task has been completed. And now that Lord Charles has confessed and has implicated the German ambassador, I'm sure he can be used to acquire something of value from Germany as they bargain for his release."

Charles turned to the King and dropped to his knees. "Your Majesty, I will not beg for your

267

forgiveness, as I deserve none. What I did was selfish, but ultimately, I thought I was doing the right thing for you and your kingdom. I realize that while I may now oppose the truce, I should have expressed those concerns rather than conspire against the Court to change the outcome of their counsel to you. I promise that I will cooperate fully in any investigation you may launch, and testify against the German ambassador. I am your loyal subject, Your Majesty."

King Philip rose, the shocked Court falling still. "While a traitor would normally be tortured then executed, should you freely reveal your secrets, then we feel torture will not be necessary." Charles stared up at the monarch, hope in his eyes. "However, your crimes cannot be forgiven. You are to be burned at the stake the day after we feel you are no longer of any use, and should satisfaction not be obtained from King Adolf, the German ambassador will be at your side, feeling the lick of the same flames that will consume you."

Charles was shaking, his face pale at the sentence, but still managed to speak to the avoidance of what was certain to have been a brutal torture. "Th-thank you, Your Majesty, you are most wise and compassionate."

King Philip ignored the man.

Charles turned to his wife, still on his knees. "Joanne, I'm so sorry for what I've done. I hope you can—"

She glared at him. "You better not be asking me to forgive you! It would be I burning at the stake if it weren't for Sir Marcus and my chambermaid. May you burn in Hell for what you have done!"

Charles' shoulders slumped, and he was hauled to his feet by two guards and led away, along with the German ambassador and the three men already in chains.

Marcus was about to join his men when the King beckoned him. He strode over to the throne and took a knee. "Your Majesty?"

"It would seem we once again owe you our gratitude."

Marcus bowed his head further. "I am humbled, Your Majesty, but I was merely doing my service to God and the truth."

King Philip beckoned him closer, and Marcus rose, leaning in. The King put his lips to Marcus' ear. "Don't make a habit of it. We do not enjoy being indebted to Templars." He waved him off, and Marcus quickly retreated several steps. The King rose with a flourish of robes, leaving the Court behind.

It erupted in animated discussion.

Marcus returned to his men, the tension of the past while slowly easing, and he unclenched his fist, unaware until this moment that he still gripped the coins.

Simon gestured toward the throne with his chin. "What was that about?"

"Just a message for his banker."

"Huh?"

Marcus chuckled. "I'll explain later."

"Sir Marcus." Joanne rushed up to him with a broad smile and tearstained cheeks. "Cousin." She hugged him hard, and he returned it awkwardly. She mercifully let him go then stepped back, giving him

269

his space. "I don't know how I can possibly thank you."

He dismissed her dilemma with a flick of his wrist. "There is no need. You are family, and I was merely doing my duty as a Templar."

"You are a good man," she sighed, echoing words apparently spoken by Isabelle. She stared toward the door her husband had been led out. "And now my next challenge begins."

Marcus frowned. "What do you mean?"

She looked up at him. "My husband is to be put to death. In France, that means his estate goes to his male heir. That will be his son from his first wife, who absolutely despises me, and will no doubt put me out of my own home."

"Do you have any other family?"

She shook her head. "None that survive. In fact, your brother-in-law was the only one I thought still lived." She frowned, and Beatrice took her hand. "I guess I will have to rely on the charity of others, though I fear that will not last, if it will be forthcoming at all."

Marcus regarded her, her future prospects tragic. She had been innocent in the entire affair, yet in the end, would still be punished for the crimes of her husband, through a system of heredity that favored males above all else.

His eyebrows rose with a thought. "You are welcome to come to the farm and stay with us. Your chambermaid as well. You are, after all, family." Her eyes widened at his words. "It won't be the life you are accustomed to, but it will be a life, and you will never go hungry or cold."

She threw herself into his arms once again, her shoulders shaking with sobs. "Oh, Cousin, the Lord truly did send you here to save me!"

She finally eased her grip on him, and he gently passed her back to Beatrice as Simon, David, and Jeremy grinned at him.

He ignored them, instead turning to Thomas. "And you, good sir, will you join us?"

Thomas' eyes darted about, looking anywhere but at Marcus. "Umm, I was actually thinking I might take Mrs. Thibault up on her offer of employment." Marcus tensed at the revelation. "I enjoy the city, and don't want to abandon my home that my father worked so hard to maintain."

Marcus' head slowly bobbed at the explanation. Farming wasn't for everyone, and in fact, he wasn't certain yet if it were for him. And he could understand the appeal of remaining in one's home, though he feared there might be more behind the decision than nostalgia. He regarded the gleeful Thibault for a moment, then put a hand on Thomas' shoulder. "I understand. Just don't do anything you'll regret having to confess to God on your day of judgment."

"Y-yes, sir." He stole a glance at Marcus. "Don't worry, you may yet see me at the farm."

Marcus smiled warmly at the young man. "There will always be a place for you."

De Rancourt Residence
Crécy-la-Chapelle, Kingdom of France

"I don't think she's very pleased with you."

Marcus looked up the path leading to the farm to see Isabelle standing in the doorway, her hands on her hips, her typical annoyed expression on her face.

There's no way she has amorous feelings for me.

"It's definitely love, hate like that."

David and Jeremy snickered at Simon's comment, and Marcus gave him a look, motioning slightly toward the two ladies riding behind them. "Mind the company we now keep."

Simon grunted. "Soon the women will outnumber us, at the rate we're taking in refugees."

Marcus laughed. "And to make things worse, quarters for them will need to be built before they are for you lot."

Jeremy groaned. "That's it. I'm sleeping in the barn."

Marcus chuckled. "I'm thinking perhaps we expand the house so that Lady Joanne and Beatrice have their own rooms, but I'm sure someone will have an opinion on that."

He smiled at Isabelle, but she stared past him, her ire directed thankfully elsewhere.

"And just where did you two run off to? I came back here to find blood, arrows, a ransacked home, and none of you in sight!"

Marcus turned in his saddle for a better view of David and Jeremy, both crimson, their heads hung in shame.

"Umm, I, umm," was all David could manage, which was better than Jeremy's feeble shoulder shrug.

Joanne rose to their defense. "You'll have to forgive them, my dear, I'm afraid we had to leave in a hurry."

Isabelle glared at her for a moment, then shook her head, jabbing a finger at David then Jeremy. "Next time, you leave a note!"

David nodded, then stared at her, wide-eyed. "Umm, can you read?"

She rushed toward him, shaking a fist, causing David to pull his horse back several paces, the others laughing. Isabelle softened her expression, turning her attention to Joanne.

"I trust all is now resolved?"

Joanne dismounted. "Yes."

"Then why are you here?"

"Unfortunately, the resolution meant destitution."

"Oh, dear." She took Joanne by the hand. "Let's get you inside, and you can tell me all about it."

Marcus watched the three women head toward their humble home, then smiled as three little ones bolted from the doorway the moment Isabelle, who had evidently told them to stay inside otherwise dire consequences would result, disappeared. He dismounted and gave them all big hugs.

"So, were you good?"

"Yes, sir," replied his nephew, Jacques.

"And you didn't pinch your sister?"

He shook his head. "No, sir."

Marcus looked at Angeline. "Is he telling the truth?"

"Yes, sir, he's much better behaved now that you're here."

Marcus laughed, patting them both on the head. "And you, Pierre, how are you faring?"

"Quite well, sir."

"Good, good. Now, why don't you go inside while we get settled."

"Yes, sir!" they cried, rushing back toward the humble home, Tanya following.

Marcus led his horse toward the barn, the others beside him, a smile on his face as the tension of the past several days slowly eased. He was home. It surprised him to think of this strange place in such a way, but nevertheless, it was indeed how he found himself thinking of this farm he had never seen a month ago.

"There's one thing I don't understand."

Marcus glanced over at Simon. "What's that?"

"How did you know it was Lord Charles? I mean, you already knew where you wanted me to send the Templar contingent to that night, and you had Sir Denys meet us at the very spot with the King's Personal Guard." He shook his head. "How could you have possibly known it was him?"

Marcus smiled. "Do you really want to know? You might feel the fool."

Simon grunted. "I already feel the fool, why not confirm it?"

Marcus chuckled. "It was the captain of Lord Charles' guard himself who revealed the truth that first day."

"I don't understand."

"Because you're a fool!"

Simon shook a fist at David who hopped out of reach.

Marcus explained. "Do you remember what he said when he was leaving, after we bested him and his men?"

Simon shrugged. "He threatened you, I think. I can't remember exactly what was said."

"He said, 'you have become involved in something far more dangerous than you can possibly imagine, and one lone knight will not be able to stop what has already begun.'"

Simon's eyes widened. "That's right!" They narrowed. "But what does that mean?"

"Think about it. At this point, all he should have known was that his master had ordered him to retrieve his wife, who had been accused of adultery. The formal charges weren't even laid until the next day, and it wasn't until then that we knew there were three others. Why would he describe this domestic issue as something far more dangerous than I could possibly imagine? I paid it little mind at the time, but once we met with Lord Charles, and I realized that all that was going on was a case of a wife being accused of adultery, his captain's warning made no sense. And as the events unfolded, and what he said began to fit the new facts, I realized there was only one reason for him to say what he had—he knew about the conspiracy.

"Lord Charles must have brought him into his confidence, as he would have needed help from time to time over the months, help from someone he could trust to have his best interests at heart, as opposed to someone supplied by the German ambassador. In so doing, he ended up revealing he was involved the moment his captain's loose tongue betrayed him in a display of false bravado aimed at trying to strike fear in the heart of an enemy who had humiliated him not moments before."

Simon shook his head. "It's a good thing you were here. If he had said that to me, I never would have remembered, and the plan could have succeeded."

"Fortunately, we have only one fool in the group."

Simon shoved David into Jeremy, sending him tumbling down the hill. Marcus laughed, turning toward his beet red squire, then staring down at the farmhouse, Lady Joanne's chambermaid already outside, collecting dried laundry, her mistress visible through the window, her laughter and that of Isabelle's carrying across the fields. He smiled then stared up at the heavens.

This wasn't the path I would have chosen for myself, Lord, but I think it will be a good one.

Simon stared up at the sky. "What are you looking at?"

Marcus laughed. "Nothing my friend, nothing. Just enjoying the fresh air of our new home."

Simon kicked the dirt then stopped, a smile spreading. "Hey, I just thought of a perk to farming, over the Holy Land."

Marcus turned to him. "Really? What?"
"There's not a stinking fish in sight."

THE END

ACKNOWLEDGMENTS

The idea for this book came to me while working on the first book in this series. While doing some research, I stumbled upon the account of the Tour de Nesle Affair, and was enthralled by what had happened. In fact, when I sat down to write this book, I had intended to use it as the basis for my story, but was halted by one inconvenient fact.

It happened in 1314, and the events of our heroes take place in 1297.

No problem. This is, after all, a work of fiction, and I instead used the true story of this affair as inspiration. And while the idea of men hiring others to impregnate their wives to produce a male heir might seem repugnant to us, heredity was so important during this time, that such things did occur, and the Tour de Nesle aftermath was the proof it could sometimes be necessary.

A 340-year dynasty collapsed as a result.

As usual, there are people to thank. My dad, as always, for the research, Susan "Miss Boss" Turnbull for some grammar help, as well as Isabelle Laprise-Enright and Chris Leroux for some French help. And, of course, my wife, daughter, mother, and friends, for their continued support, and a special thanks to the proofreading and launch teams!

To those who have not already done so, please visit my website at www.jrobertkennedy.com, then sign up for the Insider's Club to be notified of new